W9-BRA-194

DERIK'S BANE

MaryJanice Davidson

BERKLEY SENSATION, NEW YORK

THE BERKLEY PUBLISHING GROUP
Published by the Penguin Group
Penguin Group (USA) Inc.
375 Hudson Street, New York, New York 10014, USA
Penguin Group (Canada), 10 Alcorn Avenue, Toronto, Ontario M4V 3B2, Canada
(a division of Pearson Penguin Canada Inc.)
Penguin Books Ltd, 80 Strand, London WC2R 0RL, England
Penguin Group Ireland, 25 St. Stephen's Green, Dublin 2, Ireland (a division of Penguin Books Ltd.)
Penguin Group (Australia), 250 Camberwell Road, Camberwell, Victoria 3124, Australia
(a division of Pearson Australia Group Pty. Ltd.)
Penguin Books India Pvt. Ltd., 11 Community Centre, Panchsheel Park, New Delhi—110 017, India
Penguin Group (NZ), Cnr. Airborne and Rosedale Roads, Albany, Auckland 1310, New Zealand
(a division of Pearson New Zealand Ltd.)
Penguin Books (South Africa) (Pty.) Ltd., 24 Sturdee Avenue, Rosebank, Johannesburg 2196, South Africa

Penguin Books Ltd., Registered Offices: 80 Strand, London WC2R 0RL, England

This is a work of fiction. Names, characters, places, and incidents either are the product of the author's imagination or are used fictitiously, and any resemblance to actual persons, living or dead, business establishments, events, or locales is entirely coincidental.

DERIK'S BANE

A Berkley Sensation Book / published by arrangement with the author

PRINTING HISTORY
Berkley Sensation edition / January 2005

Copyright © 2005 by MaryJanice Davidson Alongi.
Excerpt from *Undead and Unappreciated* copyright © 2005 by MaryJanice Davidson Alongi.
Cover design by Pamela Jaber.
Interior text design by Stacy Irwin.

All rights reserved.
No part of this book may be reproduced, scanned, or distributed in any printed or electronic form without permission. Please do not participate in or encourage electronic piracy of copyrighted materials in violation of the author's rights. Purchase only authorized editions.
For information address: The Berkley Publishing Group,
a division of Penguin Group (USA) Inc.,
375 Hudson Street, New York, New York 10014.

ISBN: 0-425-19997-5

BERKLEY® SENSATION
Berkley Sensation Books are published by The Berkley Publishing Group,
a division of Penguin Group (USA) Inc.,
375 Hudson Street, New York, New York 10014.
BERKLEY SENSATION and the "B" design
are trademarks belonging to Penguin Group (USA) Inc.

PRINTED IN THE UNITED STATES OF AMERICA

10 9 8 7 6 5 4 3 2 1

If you purchased this book without a cover, you should be aware that this book is stolen property. It was reported as "unsold and destroyed" to the publisher, and neither the author nor the publisher has received any payment for this "stripped book."

For Giselle McKenzie,
who has been waiting for this book for years.
And for my husband, who hasn't.

Acknowledgments

Thanks as always to my family, who willingly shares me with the computer, and my husband, who shares the computer with me, not so willingly. Thanks also to the fans of *Love's Prisoner* and *Jared's Wolf*, who write me every week asking for Derik's story. Here it is.

"What, were you raised by wolves?"

Sara Gunn, R.N., Ph.D., Sorceress

"Uh . . ."

Derik Gardner, amateur cook,
werewolf, Wyndham affiliation

PART ONE

Sara and Derik

PROLOGUE

THE PAST

THE MAN HAD SHORT BROWN HAIR, NEATLY trimmed. His eyes were that mold-colored shade between gray and brown, a color everyone has seen at one time or another in the back of their fridge. His skin was the color of cheap milk chocolate, and his height was supremely average.

He was dressed in a suit several shades lighter than his skin tone, a white button-down shirt, and a gray tie with brown stripes. He had a plain gold wedding band on the third finger of his left hand, although he wasn't married. He wore black wire-rimmed glasses, although his eyesight was 20/20, and his shoes had never been shined. He looked like an accountant.

He wasn't an accountant.

The man gazed through the glass at DOE, JANE, born seventy-two minutes ago. DOE, JANE was a sweetly chubby infant with a wild shock of dark red hair. DOE, JANE was apparently born surprised, because her hair stood straight up from her skull, and her small reddish brows arched above her blue, blue eyes. She opened her small, wet mouth and let out a yell the man who wasn't an accountant could hear even through the glass.

"Well?" the nurse asked. She was a floater, here at the hospital—so thought those in charge of such things—because of understaffing. In truth, her presence at the delivery of DOE, JANE had been foretold six centuries ago. As had the violent death of DOE, JANE's father just minutes before the child crowned. As had, of course, DOE, JANE herself. "Is it . . . are they right? Is that—?"

"She who will redeem us, and our king," the man replied, "yes. She is Morgan Le Fay, among us again, and this time she will do what she could not before. This time . . ." The man smiled, showing a great many white teeth. Too many, it seemed, for his average, unassuming mouth. "This time, ours will be done."

The nurse smiled back. By contrast, her smile wasn't frightening in the least—she had the grin of a beauty contestant. But her eyes were dead.

They watched DOE, JANE through the glass for a long time.

1

MICHAEL WYNDHAM STEPPED OUT OF HIS BED-
room, walked down the hall, and saw his best
friend, Derik Gardner, on the main floor headed
for the front door. He grabbed the banister and
vaulted, dropped fifteen feet, and landed with a
solid thud he felt all the way through his knees.
"Hey, Derik!" he called cheerfully. "Wait a sec!"

From his bedroom he heard his wife mutter, "I
hate when he does that . . . gives me a flippin'
heart attack every time," and couldn't help grin-
ning. Wyndham Manor had been his home all his
life, and the only time he walked up or down
those stairs was when he was carrying his daughter, Lara. He didn't know how ordinary humans

could stand walking around in their fragile little shells. He'd tried to talk to his wife about this on a few occasions, but her eyes always went flinty, and her gun hand flexed, and the phrase "hairy fascist bastard" came up, and things got awkward. Werewolves were tough, incredibly tough, but compared to Homo sapiens, who wasn't?

It was a ridiculously perfect day outside, and he couldn't blame Derik for wanting to head out as quickly as possible. Still, there was something troubling his old friend, and Michael was determined to get to the bottom of it.

"Hold up," Michael said, reaching for Derik's shoulder. "I want to—"

"I don't care what you want," Derik replied without turning. He grabbed Michael's hand and flung it away, so sharply Michael lost his balance for a second. "I'm going out."

Michael tried to laugh it off, ignoring the way the hairs on the back of his neck tried to stand up. "Touch-ee! Hey, I just want to—"

"I'm going *out*!" Derik moved, cat-quick, and then Michael was flying through the air with the greatest of ease, only to slam into the door to the coat closet hard enough to splinter it down the middle.

Michael lay on his back a moment like a stunned beetle. Then he flipped to his feet, ignoring the slashing pain down his back. "My friend," he said, "you are so right. Except you're going out on the tip of my boot, pardon me while I kick your ass." This in a tone of mild banter, but Michael was crossing the room in swift strides, barely noticing that his friend Moira, who had just come in from the kitchen, squeaked and jumped out of the way.

Best friend or no, nobody—*nobody*—knocked the alpha male around in his own . . . damned . . . house. The other Pack members lived there by his grace and favor, thanks very much, and while the forty-room house had more than enough room for them all, certain things were simply . . . not . . . done.

"Don't start with me," Derik warned. The morning sunlight was slanting through the skylight, shining so brightly it looked like Derik's hair was about to burst into flames. His friend's mouth—usually relaxed in a wiseass grin—was a tight slash. His grass-green eyes were narrow. He looked—Michael had trouble believing it—ugly and dangerous. Rogue. "Just stay off."

"You started it, at the risk of sounding junior high, and you're going to show throat and apologize, or you'll be counting your broken ribs all the way to the emergency room."

"Come near me again, and we'll see who's counting ribs."

"Derik. Last chance."

"Cut it out!" It was Moira, shrieking from a safe distance. "Don't do this in his own house, you idiot! He won't stand down, and you two morons—schmucks—losers will hurt each other!"

"Shut up," Derik said to the woman he (usually) lovingly regarded as a sister. "And get lost . . . this isn't for you."

"I'm getting the hose," she warned, "and then *you* can pay to have the floors resealed."

"Moira, out," Michael said without looking around. She was a fiercely intelligent female werewolf who could knock over an elm if she needed to, but she was no match for two males squaring off. The day was headed down the shit hole already; he wouldn't see Moira hurt on top of it. "And Derik, she's right, let's take this out-side—ooooof!"

He didn't duck, though he could see the blow coming. He should have ducked, but . . . he still couldn't believe what was happening. His best friend—Mr. Nice Guy himself!—was challenging his authority. Derik, always the one to jolly people out of a fight. Derik, who had Michael's back in every fight, who had saved his wife's life, who loved Lara like she was his own.

The blow—hard enough to shatter an ordinary man's jaw—knocked him back a full three steps. And that was that. Allowances had been made, but now the gloves were off. Moira was still shrieking, and he could sense other people filling the room, but it faded to an unimportant drone.

Derik gave up trying for the door and slowly turned. It was like watching an evil moon come over the horizon. He glared, full in the face: a dead-on challenge for dominance. Michael grabbed for his throat, Derik blocked, they grappled. A red cloud of rage swam across Michael's vision; he didn't see his boyhood friend, he saw a rival. A challenger.

Derik wasn't giving an inch, was shoving back just as hard, warning growls ripping from his throat, growls that only fed Michael's rage

(rival! rival for your mate, your cub! show throat or die!)

made him yearn to twist Derik's head off, made him want to pound, tear, hurt—

Suddenly, startlingly, a small form was between them. Was shoving, hard. Sheer surprise broke them apart.

"Daddy! Quit it!" Lara stood between them, arms akimbo. "Just . . . don't do that!"

His daughter was standing protectively in front of Derik. Not that Derik cared, or even noticed; his gaze was locked on Michael's: hot and uncompromising.

Jeannie, frozen at the foot of the stairs, let out a yelp and lunged toward her daughter, but Moira moved with the speed of an adder and flung her arms around the taller woman. This earned her a bellow of rage. "Moira, what the hell? Let go!"

"You can't interfere," was the small blonde's quiet reply. "None of us can." Although Jeannie was quite a bit taller and heavier, the smaller woman had no trouble holding Jeannie back. Jeannie was the alpha female, but human—the first human alpha the Pack had known in three hundred years. Moira would follow almost any command Jeannie might make . . . but wouldn't let the woman endanger herself, or interfere with Pack law that was as old as the family of Man.

Oblivious to the drama on the stairs, Derik started forward again, but Lara planted her feet. "Quit it, Derik!" She swung her small foot into Derik's shin, which he barely noticed. "And Daddy, you quit, too. Leave him alone. He's just sad and feeling stuck. He doesn't want to hurt you."

Michael ignored her. He was glaring at his rival and reaching for Derik again, when his daughter's voice cut through the tension like a laser scalpel. "I said *leave him alone*."

That got his attention; he looked down at her in a hurry. He expected tears, red-faced anger, but Lara's face was, if anything, too pale. Her eyes were huge, so light brown they were nearly gold. Her dark hair was pulled back in two curly pigtails.

He realized anew how tall she was for her age,

and how she was her mother's daughter. And her father's. Her gaze was direct, adult. And not a little disconcerting.

"What?" Shock nearly made him stammer. Behind him, nobody moved. It seemed nobody even breathed. And Derik was standing down, backing off, heading for the door. Michael, in light of these highly interesting new events, let him go. He employed his best Annoyed Daddy tone. "*What* did you say, Lara?"

She didn't flinch. "You heard me. But you won't hear me say it again."

He was furious, appalled. This wasn't—he had to—she couldn't—But pride was rising, blotting out the fury. Oh, his Lara! Intelligent, gorgeous—and utterly without fear! Would he have ever *dared* face down his father?

It occurred to him that the future Pack leader was giving him an order. Now what to do about it?

A long silence passed, much longer in retrospect. This would be a moment his daughter would remember if she lived to be a thousand. He could break her . . . or he could start training a born leader.

He bowed stiffly. He didn't show the back of his neck; it was the polite bow to an equal. "A wiser head has prevailed. Thank you, Lara." He turned on his heel and walked toward the stairs, catching Jeannie's hand on the way up, leaving the others behind. Moira had released her grip on his wife, was staring, openmouthed, at Lara. They were all staring. He didn't think it had ever been so quiet in the main hall.

Michael was intent on reaching his bedroom where he could think about all that had just happened, and gain his wife's counsel. He didn't quite dare go after Derik just yet—best to take time for their blood to cool. Christ! It wasn't even eight o'clock in the morning!

"Mikey—what—cripes—"

And Lara. His daughter, who jumped between two werewolves with their blood up. Who faced him down and demanded he leave off. His daughter, defending her dearest friend. His daughter, who had just turned four. They had known she was ferociously intelligent, but to have such a strong sense of what was right and what was—

Jeannie cut through his thoughts with a typically wry understatement. "This *can't* be good. But I'm sure you can explain it to me. Use hand puppets. And me without my So You Married a Werewolf guide . . ."

Then he was closing their bedroom door and thinking about his place in the Pack, and his daughter's, and how he hoped he wouldn't have to kill his best friend before the sun set.

2

DERIK HEARD THE FOOTSTEPS AND SLOWED. HE'D made it almost all the way to the beach but, unless he felt like swimming to London, it was time to stop and think with his head instead of his temper.

Whoever was approaching was downwind, so he didn't know for sure, but he braced himself for Michael. He'd have to apologize, or there would be real trouble. And he *would* apologize. He would. He owed it to his friend, and worse, he'd behaved badly. So he would apologize. Yes. Absolutely.

But it would taste like shit in his mouth.

Derik stared out to sea and shook his head at

this sorry-ass turn of events. He and Mike had grown up together. Their mothers had often put them in the same crib to nap. They had experienced their first Change the same month of the same year; he remembered Mike had been as thrilled, as terrified, as drunk on the moon as he had been. They had chased together, hunted together, killed together. Had defended the Pack together.

He had no problem with Michael; he loved the big dope.

He just didn't love Michael being the boss. Not anymore.

Derik made a fist and hit himself on the thigh. This was his problem, not Michael's, and he had to figure out how to fix it, pronto. He owed the big guy respect, not just brotherly love. And show it he would, no matter how the words wanted to choke him. He wasn't some—some monkey, fighting for the sake of it. He was a werewolf, member of the Wyndham Pack, and fully grown besides. Squabbling was beneath him. So was picking fights.

He turned, forcing a smile . . . and the clod of

dirt hit him right in the middle of the forehead. It exploded, and dust sprayed everywhere.

"Idiot! Putz! Dumb ass!"

"Jeez, Moira," he complained, secretly glad showing throat had been put off a bit, "you could have put my eye out."

"I was *aiming* for your eye, you stupid asshole!"

"Now, Moira, you know you shouldn't use such vague terms," he teased. "You gotta speak in black and white, honey, really let people know what's on your mind."

She wasn't having it; the scowl didn't crack. She marched the rest of the way up to him—looking cute as hell in khaki shorts and a lavender T-shirt—and kicked him smartly in the shin. It hurt, too; Moira had toenails like a sloth. "How could you risk your life like that? We nearly had a fight for dominance in the main hall in front of all your friends. In front of Lara! You're lucky Michael didn't tear your head off. You're lucky Jeannie didn't shoot you!"

He didn't want to, but couldn't help it: He felt his lips draw back from his teeth. "I could have taken him."

Moira threw up her hands. "What is *wrong* with you? You've been like a hungry bear all summer. This is a good time for us, Derik— Michael's brought peace, Gerald's gone, we caught the monster who'd been killing those poor girls . . . there's never been a better time to be a werewolf. So why are you trying so hard to screw things up?"

He looked at her, this fine woman, as dear to him as Michael was. *Oh, yeah?* a treacherous inner voice whispered. *Dear to you, huh? You've got a funny way of showing it, jerkoff.*

He didn't have an answer for her. "I don't know what's wrong," he said dully. "I just want to fight, all the time. Everything that comes out of Michael's mouth is pissing me off. I love him, but I could choke him right now just to watch his eyeballs bulge."

Moira's own eyeballs bulged a bit at that, but she recovered quickly. Her eyes—so fine a blue they were nearly lavender—went narrow and thoughtful. She began to pace, looking not unlike a petite blonde general.

"Okay, well, let's figure this out." He smiled in spite of himself. Moira the math genius. Every problem could be broken down to an equation and, thus, solved. Well, hell, she'd figured out where Bin Laden was hiding, hadn't she? Luckily for the world, one of the cabinet members was a werewolf. Moira had sent an E-mail, and forty-eight hours later, hello, spider hole. "Are you in love with Jeannie?"

"Wha—no!"

"Okay, calm down. It's an explanation, you know . . . if you wanted another man's mate."

"Well, I don't. I mean, I *like* her and all, but she's Michael's. Just like he's hers. You can't really picture either of them with anyone else, can you?"

Moira stopped pacing and smiled at him. "No, you're right about that. All right, then," she continued matter-of-factly, "are you in love with me?"

"Ewww, no!"

Unfortunately, she kept going. "Are you upset because I've taken a mate and am having sex with him pretty much every chance I—"

"Aagghh, Moira, please, my eardrums are gonna implode!"

She arched her brows. " 'Eww'?"

"Honey, you're too cute to be believed, but I have never—*never*, yuck!—thought of you that way. Never. Ugh! Did I say never?"

"All right, you don't have to induce vomiting to get your point across."

"If it'll get your mind off that track . . ." he warned, fully prepared to shove a finger down his throat.

"Well, it's another theory, that's all."

"A bad, terrible, awful, yucky theory. Baby, we grew up together. You're like the sister I never wanted." He flopped down onto the sand to watch her pace. "Don't take this the wrong way or anything, but if you put your tongue in my mouth, I'd probably barf."

"Mutual, wise guy. Actually, I was sure you were picking a fight because you've got the urge to settle down with a mate, and you're surrounded by mated couples, and . . . well, I know how you feel, is all." She paused, looking pensive. "I was so lonesome before Jared came."

"Moira mated with a monkey, Moira mated with a monkey," Derik sang.

"Shut up, don't call him that! God, I really hate that term."

"I dare you to use it in front of Jeannie," he teased.

"Do I look like I want to spend the rest of the day in an iron lung? Never mind the humans in our lives . . . my point is, I couldn't stand to be around Michael or Jeannie, because seeing their happiness made me feel worse. I figured that was your problem, too."

"Well, it's not. Don't get me wrong, cutie, I'd love to find the right girl and knock her up—"

"And cherish and love her," Moira added dryly.

"—but I've got time. Hell, I'm not even thirty yet."

"Well, we could see if Michael—"

"Leave him out of this."

She chewed on her lower lip for a moment, then adopted an overly innocent expression that put him instantly on guard. The last time she'd looked like that, she had encouraged Lara to cut up his cashmere sweater to make soft puppets. "We should talk to Michael, you know. He's our leader. He'll tell us what to do."

He ground his teeth in irritation. "Moira, whatever the problem is, *I will figure it out.* I don't need Michael shoving his snout in where it's not wanted."

"But he'll fix everything. He'll tell you how to solve your problem, and you'll listen to him, and you'll be better."

"I said I can handle this *by myself*!"

"You don't want his help?"

He bounced to his feet so swiftly, to a human it would have looked like he teleported. "Jesus, do I have to write it on my forehead? Whatever it is, it's my problem, not his, so he should just *leave me be!*"

"Ah," she said quietly. "So that's it. Also, back up before I bite off your chin."

He did, realizing he and Moira were nose-to-nose. As nose-to-nose as they could be, anyway—he was a foot taller. "Sorry. I should probably take a walk, sweetie, I'm not good company right now."

"I wonder when it happened?"

"When *what* happened?" he practically snarled.

"When you became alpha."

"Don't be ridiculous," he said automatically, but inwardly he could feel himself nodding.

"Oh," she said, watching him, "and you knew, of course. Sure. You knew, but you ignored it, because you don't want to hurt anyone, and you don't want to leave us. Why would you? You've lived here all your life—we all have. This is home."

He stared at her. Moira, so pretty and cute and helpless-looking . . . Moira, the most intuitive person he'd ever met. "Sometimes you're scary, you know?"

She smirked. "Of course." Her smile dropped away. "I'm only annoyed I didn't figure it out sooner. But Derik . . . as you know perfectly well, one Pack cannot support two alphas. It just can't. That's why there are fights for dominance. That's why you have to leave. Now. Today."

"But Moira, I—"

"Now. *Today.* Before this gets worse and you do something we'll all regret, forever." She softened her brisk tone and gently touched his brow. "Because if you or Michael died . . . none of us could bear it."

She didn't add what they both knew. If Michael killed Derik, she would leave. And if Derik killed Michael, she would kill him—try, anyway—and leave. Would the Pack hold? Sure. It had been around for centuries and had been through much worse than the squabbles of alpha males. Would the Pack be a place of love and light any longer?

No.

He didn't dare say a word. She was speaking exact truths, her specialty, and though he could hardly stand to hear the words, he'd ignored the problem long enough. But if he spoke, he'd probably burst into tears like a kid and embarrass them both. He hadn't cried since his mother died, but these thoughts had been heavy on his heart for the last few months.

"Derik, the wolf in you wants the Pack. But the man in you would never forgive himself if he took it."

Still he said nothing, but she stepped closer, and he rested his forehead on her shoulder. They stood that way, motionless on the beach, for a long time.

3

"AAAAAAGGGGGG—"

"I'm really sorry—"

"—gggggggggggghhhhhhhhhh—"

"—but the transmission's completely shot—"

"—gggggggggggghhhhhhhhhh—"

"—and we'll have to keep the car for at least a week—"

"—gggggggggggghhhhhhhhhh—"

"—while we work on it—"

"—gggggggggggghhhhhhhhhh—"

"—it'll cost a little more than the estimate I gave you . . . Christ, lady, take a breath, will ya?"

Sara Gunn sagged against something large and greasy—not the mechanic—and concentrated on not passing out. New transmission! Eighty zillion dollars to fix, and meanwhile no car for at least a week! Now the mechanic would gouge out her eyes and make her catch up on her laundry, and the day would be complete.

"We coulda caught it earlier if you had more than two oil changes a year," the mechanic ("Dave" was emblazoned on his shirt pocket) said with mild reproach. "Ask me how to save on your next tire rotation!" was on his T-shirt in migraine-inducing yellow. Sara disliked lectures from men who wore instructions on their clothing.

"I hate bringing my car to the garage," she muttered. She could feel the clammy sweat of panic beginning to bead between her shoulder blades.

"How come?"

"Because I always get expensive news!" she snapped. "Look. I'm sorry. I know it's not your fault. It was a shock, and I don't handle surprises well."

"How could you be surprised? Your car's an automatic, but it doesn't change gears unless you hold the accelerator down for at least ten seconds—"

"Well, it started okay, so I didn't think much of it."

"And the cruise control locks up on you all the time—didn't you say the car forced you through a school zone at seventy miles an hour?"

"Hey, it was Sunday at ten o'clock at night, all right? It's not like there were kids around." He frowned at her and she flushed. "Well, that's why I brought it in."

"M' point is, you got no cause to be shocked that it's an expensive problem. You're exactly like a gal who finds a lump in her tit but won't go to the tit doc and then gets pissed when he tells her she has cancer," Dave pronounced. "I see it all the time."

"First of all, that's the worst analogy I've ever heard. Second, I'm not paying you to lecture me."

"Actually, you ain't paid me at all," he pointed out with a grin. She could be cute, if you liked them rangy and curvy and red-haired, which he surely did. "Nope, not a cent."

"Well, I'm going to, okay? Hell, your kids will

go to Harvard thanks to my stupid transmission." On "stupid," she kicked her rear left tire.

"Ha! Harvard. I coulda gone," he confided, "but I didn't want to live on the other coast."

"Trust me, it was overrated." Sara sighed and ran her fingers through her too-long bangs. If hair that grew past your chin could be considered bangs. "Well, as long as you're doing the transmission thing, see what you can do about the clock. It goes off when I turn on my headlights."

"It does?"

"Yes. But as soon as I turn my lights off, it comes right back on, except then it's wrong, and I have to adjust the time until the next time I turn on my headlights. Also, I lost the car lighter—"

"How could you lose—?"

"I just looked down one day and it was gone, all right? Why don't you get a spotlight and shine it into my eyes? Anyway, every once in a while sparks will shoot out from the lighter, which is kind of distracting."

"I guess so."

"My horn doesn't work, either."

"Now, how did that happen?"

She ignored the question. "Also, my radio only

gets the local pop station. Which wouldn't be so bad, but they play about six Lenny Kravitz songs each hour." She sighed again. "I used to like Lenny Kravitz."

Dave blinked slowly, like a lizard. "Why haven't you bought a new car?"

"It was my mom's car," she said simply. "She loved the wretched thing."

"Oh." He gnawed his lower lip a moment. Everybody in town knew what had happened to Mrs. Gunn. Nobody talked about it. He'd have felt sorry for her even if she wasn't such a dolly. And Sara *was* cute, with those crystal blue eyes and the flyaway mass of red curls. Her skin was perfectly white, like fresh cream . . . not a freckle in sight. He figured if she ever set foot on a tropical beach, she'd go up in flames.

"Look, Dr. Gunn, I'm sorry to be the bringer of bad news to you and stuff, but I'll get your car in as quick as I can. Shouldn't take more than a few days."

"A few days of purgatory!" she shouted, startling him. That was another thing about Dr. Gunn. You'd be having a perfectly normal conversation with the woman, when she'd start screaming. It was true about the temperament of redheads, and that was a fact.

"Meantime, I got a loaner I can let you have for"—at least forty a day, or his boss would kill him. Okay, thirty. Twenty-five ninety-five and that was his final offer—"for nothing. On account of you getting such a bad shock and all."

She smiled and he nearly fell back into the tire pile. She was cute when she was ranting and fussing and being a pain. She was completely gorgeous when she smiled. Her dimples popped into view, and her eyes crinkled at the corners and made you wonder what her mouth would taste like.

He smiled back.

What are you doing, Davey old pal? You got as much chance with Dr. Sara Gunn as you've got to grow tits and fly away.

"That'd be great, Dave," she said with real warmth. "I'm sorry about the tantrum."

"It's not the first one I've seen. You gotta temper on you like a rabid polecat." He said this with total admiration.

"Uh . . . thank you."

"Maybe after your car is fixed, we could have dinner?"

"Of course! And it'll be my treat, for the free loaner." She smiled at him again. The way she smiled at her students, her colleagues, love-struck mechanics. Dr. Gunn was brainy, high-strung, occasionally shrill, and had no freakin' clue she was a stone knockout.

"Thanks," he sighed. *Ehh. Worth a shot.* "I'll call you when I get an idea how long it'll take."

"Thanks again."

He ended up giving her the nicest loaner he had, a silver 2004 Dodge Stratus. His boss would strangle him like a rooster when he found out what he'd done.

Screw it.

"YOU HAVE TO SAVE THE WORLD."

Derik fought to keep his jaw from dropping. "Me?"

"Yes, brain-drain, you. In fact, could you get started on that right away?"

Moira clapped her hands. "A quest! Just what you needed, oh, it's perfect, perfect!"

"A quest? Do I look like a Hobbit to you? *I* have to save the world? From what?"

Antonia smirked. "From who, actually."

"From whom, actually," Moira corrected.

Antonia glared at her. Moira stared back, eyebrows arched, and after a moment the taller woman dropped her gaze. Antonia was one of those rare human/werewolf hybrids, but nobody liked her much. Born of a human father and a were mother, she couldn't Change, though she had the preternatural strength and speed common to their kind.

Being unable to Change had been a tremendous burden on her as a child . . . the Pack expected much from its hybrids. Her parents tried—and failed—to hide their despair. Hers had not been an easy adolescence, as much from the tremendous pressure she put on herself, as anything ever said, or intimated. "The only thing I have going for me," she often said with bitter insight, "are my looks. And around here, gorgeous bims are a dime a dozen."

This was true. No one was sure if it was breeding or genetics or great good fortune or the omnivore diet, but werewolves, in addition to being exceptionally strong and exceptionally fast, were exceptionally easy on the eyes. Antonia had enormous dark eyes and creamy skin, long legs and the figure of a swimsuit model, but it didn't set her apart.

Nobody had a clue what Antonia was until she woke up the morning of her seventeenth birthday, made herself toast and poached eggs, then fell over in a dead faint. When she regained consciousness, she brushed the egg out of her hair and told her astonished parents, "Michael's going to get someone pregnant today, will be married by summertime and a father before Easter. Oh," she added thoughtfully, "the baby will be a girl, and the epidural won't work for the mom-to-be. Hee!"

To everyone's amazement, she had been right. It was the first of dozens of predictions, some mild ("Moira's going to get stuck with another audit . . . ha!"), some major ("Stay the hell out of New York on September 11, 2001."). She was never wrong. She was never even off a little bit. No one had seen anything like it. No one was even sure what it meant—could werewolves harness mental power as well as physical? It was a mystery to all.

And overnight, Antonia had gone from Pack Nobody to Pack Demigod. Piss her off, and nothing might happen . . . or she might foresee your death and fail to warn you, out of spite.

Now here she was, holding court in the solarium, explaining that the world was going to end unless Derik made it to 6 Fairy Lane, Monterey, California, as soon as possible.

"You guys know who Morgan Le Fay is?"

Moira nodded. Derik blinked. "Guess I'll play dumb blonde," he said, avoiding Moira's poke. "No idea."

"She was the half sister of King Arthur," Antonia explained. "She had an incestuous affair with her brother and was responsible, indirectly, for his death. She was also a powerful sorceress."

"Uh-huh. That's fascinating, hon. I like story time as much as the next fella, but this is relevant because . . . ?"

"I got a line on her."

"A line on her," Moira repeated. "Toni, what in God's name are you talking about?"

"An-TON-ee-uh. And Morgan Le Fay is in Monterey Bay."

"You're a poet, and you don't know it," Derik joked, and was unsurprised to see both women ignore him.

"She's reincarnated and goes by the name of Dr. Sara Gunn. You have to get over there and take care of her. If you don't, a week from now none of us will be here."

Dead silence, broken by Moira's faint, "Oh, Antonia . . . for real?"

"No, I made it all up because I want the attention," she snapped. "Yes! The world's gonna end, and we're all fucked, unless the Pack's answer to The Rock gets his ass in gear."

Another brief silence, and then Moira said, "I think—I think I'd better go get Michael and Jeannie."

For once, Derik didn't argue.

MICHAEL CLEARED HIS THROAT FROM THE DOORway. "You're going, then?"

Derik straightened up from his packing. He'd tossed a few things into a carry-on and was ready to leave. More than ready. He was taking the Wyndham jet to San Jose, California, and from there he'd pick up a rental car to the Monterey Peninsula. He'd already said good-bye to Moira and Jeannie.

"Yeah, I'm going now. In fact, I'd better get a move on."

"Well. Be careful. Don't let her get the drop on you."

"The reincarnation of the most powerful sorceress in the history of literature, fated to destroy the world in the next few days? No chance," he bragged, and was relieved to see a ghost of a grin on Michael's face. "Leave it to me. This'll be just like the time I agreed to cater your mating ceremony. Except with less flour."

"I am leaving it to you," Michael said seriously. "You knew Jeannie was pregnant again, right?"

He nodded. They all knew.

"Well, for God's sake, don't tell her you knew before I told you," Michael said hastily. "I had the worst time pretending to be surprised when she finally got around to breaking the news. And, of course, she knew I wasn't surprised, and then the shit hit the fan."

"It's not your fault you can smell it on her," he said, puzzled.

"You'd think. Anyway . . . my point is . . . everything I have, and am, is in your hands. It's too bad—" *We haven't been getting along* was the obvious end to that statement, but his friend was too tactful to say it.

"Yeah. Don't worry, chief."

Michael smiled again. "I'm not. Well, I am, a little—it's how I'm made. But, hell, if anyone can save the world, you can. I'd bet my life on it." He paused. "I *am* betting my life on it."

Derik was too gratified to speak for a moment. He remembered his earlier words—his earlier actions—and felt his face burn with shame. So he wanted his own Pack—or at least, wanted to be his own man. Did that mean he had to treat his best friend like something to be scraped off the bottom of his shoe?

"Uh . . . thanks . . . but before I go . . ." He slung his bag over one shoulder, crossed the room, and started to hunch lower, prepared to show throat.

Michael grasped his shoulder and jerked him back up. "Don't do that," he said quietly. "For one thing, you're off to save the world, so as far as I'm concerned, the slate's clean between us. For another, Moira says you could be alpha. Since I'm pretty sure she's never been wrong about anything—"

"It's annoying," Derik agreed.

"—it's best for you to get out of the habit of showing throat as soon as possible."

Derik paused. "So . . . we almost had to cha-cha today, but because I'm gonna save the world, you're gonna let that go?"

"That's just the kind of swell guy I am," Michael said solemnly, and both men cracked up, their laughter sounding more like howls than anything else.

5

THE MONTEREY PENINSULA

HE KNEW IT MADE HIM SHALLOW. HE KNEW HE WAS
probably too old for such nonsense. He knew he
should be focused on saving the world. But he
couldn't help it.

Derik loved convertibles. And this one was
sublime—electric, eye-watering blue, with leather
seats and a superb sound system. Robert Palmer's
"Addicted to Love" was tearing his head off, because, joy of joys, he'd found a local all-eighties
rock radio station. The weather was gorgeous—
low 70s and sunny—and his proximity to the
ocean meant that thousands and thousands of
tantalizing scents were on the air.

He took a gulp and dizzily tried to process.

Derik's nose was an instrument of frightening precision, but even it could be confused and overwhelmed. Shit, that was half the fun of a convertible! Right now he was smelling seaspray-lilacshottarmacdeerpoopraccoonsseagullfeathers—whoops! Now he was getting a tantalizing whiff of fishoceangrasslawnmowerexhaustpossumfriedchicken and—thank you, Jesus!—girlsweat and Dune perfume.

I am in California, land of babes and cool cars and movies-of-the-week, but I can't think about that until I save the world.

At the thought of what was riding on this little day trip, his heart lurched. He had always thought of himself as a mellow kind of fellow (recent events notwithstanding), and if someone had told him he'd be responsible for saving the world—not the Pack, or even his closest friends, but the *world*, the *entire world* . . . well, his mind just couldn't get around it. It would try, and then it would veer away and think about something stupid, like how great it was to find an eighties radio station so far from home.

Saying good-bye to Lara did it. Brought it home for him, however briefly. He loved that little stinker like she was his own pup. He'd die for her in a New York minute. He'd wring the neck of anybody who hurt her and snap the spine of anyone who made her cry. But if he fucked up— if this Morgan gal got away from him—Lara would never make it to first grade. Never go on a date, never experience her first Change. Never grow up to be his boss, the way her daddy was.

Shit, he'd almost burst out crying just saying good-bye to her.

Quickest done, quickest back home. Not that he was so terribly anxious to go back home—the mansion held its own unique set of problems. Derik figured you knew your life was screwed up when you were almost glad you could use saving the world as a distraction.

Well. He and Mike would work shit out. They had to. Otherwise—otherwise, he just would never go home again, even though that probably wasn't the best way to handle things.

He didn't trust himself around Mike, that was all. If he lost his temper and things got way out of hand, the deed would be done, and Mike would be dead, and he'd be Pack leader, and Jeannie would be a widow, and Lara would be without a daddy, and then he'd probably go off in a corner and blow his brains out. Better to be a *(coward)* loner than risk that. Way better.

SARA GUNN THRUST HER FOOT INTO THE SECOND pair of panty hose of the morning and, incredibly, had the same thing happen. There was a zizzzzzzzz! sound, and then her big toenail ripped a runner through her last pair of panty hose.

"Right," she grumbled. "Why is it that when I'm running late, everything goes wrong? More important, why am I talking to myself?" She jerked the nylon torture chamber off her foot and flung it over her shoulder to the floor. "Okay, then . . . it's gorgeous out. A perfect day to go bare-legged." She ran a hand down her left leg. A little raspy, but hardly Yosemite Sam whiskers. *Note to self: Shave legs more often when low on panty hose.*

She heard the doorbell, that annoying dum-DUM-dum-dum . . . dum-DUM-dum . . . dum-DUM-dum-dum-DUM! Dah-dum-dah-dum-dum. She cursed her late mother's infatuation with Alex Trebek and *Jeopardy.* Every time she had a visitor, she felt like phrasing everything in the form of a question.

I will never see twenty-five again . . . or twenty-eight, for that matter, and I never quite managed to move out of my mother's house. Nice one, Gunn. Not pathetic at all!

She slipped her feet into a pair of low-heeled pumps and squinted distractedly at the mirror. Hair: presentable, if not exactly glamorous, caught up in one of those big black clips that looked like a medieval torture device. Skin: too pale; no time for makeup. Eyes: big and blue and bloodshot—damn that *Deep Space Nine* marathon, anyway. Suit: cream linen, which meant she'd be a wrinkled mess in another hour. Legs: bare. Feet: narrow and stuffed into shoes so pointy, she could see the crack between her first and second toe.

"Too bad, my girl!" she told herself. "Next time don't hit the snooze button so many times."

Dum-DUM-dum-dum . . . dum-DUM-dum . . . dum-DUM-dum-dum-DUM! Dah-dum-dah-dum-dum.

"Be right there!" She hurried out of her bedroom, glanced through the kitchen, and breathed a sigh of relief at the sight of the loaner car. Finally! David, her mechanic, had at last had a chance to send over a loaner car for her use. A flashy loaner car, at that. Well, beggars can't be . . . et cetera. The other loaner had conked out after an hour—was it her fault she couldn't drive a stick?

She flung the door open. "Thank goodness you're—whoa."

She stared at the man standing on her front porch. He was, to be blunt, delicious. He was to Homo sapiens what a hot fudge sundae was to vanilla ice cream: a complete and total improvement on the original. A full head taller than she was, he practically filled the door frame. His blond hair was the color of sunlight, of ripe wheat, of—of something really gorgeous. He had swimmers' shoulders and she could actually see the definition of his stomach muscles through the green T-shirt he wore. The shirt had the puzzling logo "Martha Rocks" in bright white letters. He was wearing khaki shorts, revealing heavily muscled legs tapering into absurdly large feet, sockless in a pair of battered loafers. His hands, she noticed, were also quite large, with squared off fingers and blunt, short nails.

He was lightly tanned and had the look of a man equally at home camping in the woods, lounging poolside, or hunched over a computer. His eyes were the brilliant green of wet leaves, and they sparkled with turbulence and lusty good humor. His mouth was wide and mobile and looked made for smiling.

He was smiling at *her*.

Get a grip, she ordered herself. She was annoyed to find her pulse was racing. *It is unbelievably juvenile to be panting at this man, when all he's done is ring your bell twice and stand there. He hasn't even opened his mouth and you're practically a puddle on your own doorstep. He—oh, oh! He's talking!*

"—wrong house."

"What did you say?"

"I said, I must have the wrong house." His smile widened, as his gaze raked her from head to foot, taking in her bare legs, scuffed shoes, rumpled suit, and messy hair. His teeth were perfectly straight, almost blindingly white, and looked sharp. The guy probably ate his steak raw. He could make a fortune doing Chiclets commercials. "I'm sorry to bother you."

"No, you've got the right house. I've been waiting for the loaner." She nodded at the flashy little blue convertible. "The other profs are going to accuse me of entering my midlife crisis a little early, but what can you do? Come in. How are you getting back to the garage?"

He stepped inside, and as she reached past him to shut the screen door, she was reminded all over again—as if she needed it!—just how large he was. She was not a petite woman by any means—in fact, she ought to lay off the chocolate croissants—but he made her feel absolutely tiny. She caught a sniff of him and nearly purred. He smelled like soap and male. Big, clean male.

He glanced around her kitchen. "Listen, I don't want to put you out, but can you tell me which house is number 6 Fairy Lane?"

"It's this one," she said with bare impatience. Gorgeous, but not terribly bright. Well, nobody was perfect. "I told you, you're in the right place. I'm running late for rounds, so if you could just arrange to have someone pick you up—"

"Yeah, I'll do that. 'Cuz there's obviously been a mistake."

"Tell me about it," she said, looking at him

with longing. In a perfect world, he would be her pool boy. Instead, she was late for work and he had to hitch a ride back to his place of business. "Well, thanks for dropping off the car—see you."

He followed her onto the porch. "It was nice meeting you. Sorry about the misunderstanding." But, interestingly, instead of being regretful, he sounded weirdly relieved.

Odd! But, she had no time to ponder it. "Bye!"

She got the car going with no trouble—she'd heard the phrase "the engine purred like a kitten" before but had no real experience with it until now—and pulled out of the driveway. She waved to the man who should have been her pool boy, who was looking as though he'd had a touch of sun, and dropped the pedal.

6.

DERIK WENT TO THE NEAREST SAFE HOUSE, THE one down the block from the aquarium. An adorable cub answered the door, a boy about eight years old with big dark eyes and black hair.

"Hi," Derik said. "Are your folks home?"

"Sure. What's your name?"

"Derik."

"Okay. Come on in."

Derik followed the boy into a kitchen that smelled like cookie dough and found the lady of the house up to her elbows in butterscotch chips. "Well, hi there," she said, her greeting a soft Midwestern twang. "My name's Marjie Wolfton; this is my son, Terry. Do you need some help?"

"Just a private phone. I'm—uh—sort of on a mission to—um—never mind." He just couldn't bring himself to say "save the world." It was too bizarre.

Marjie, however, seemed to know all about it. Either that, or she was used to strange werewolves showing up at her door. "Yes, of course. Terry, show Derik the den."

"Okay." The boy snatched a fistful of dough and disappeared down a hallway. Derik followed him into the den, which had a hardwood floor, windows set into the ceiling, a computer, a phone, and a television.

"Are you from Massachusetts?" Terry asked.

"Uh-huh." He was going to have to call Antonia and figure out this mess. No way was that distracted cutie Morgan Le Fay. *No* way. "How'd you know? Am I dropping my Rs?"

The boy ignored the question. "And you live with Michael Wyndham? The Pack leader?"

Derik looked at the boy, really looked. That was pure hero worship, if he wasn't mistaken. And since he used to think of Michael's father in the exact same way, Derik completely understood where the kid was coming from. Men who took a Pack . . . ran a Pack . . . they were just . . . different. More *there*. And they could make you like them. It was a talent, the way some people could raise just one eyebrow. It was hard to explain.

"Yeah, I live out there with those guys. Michael's my best friend." Was? Is? *Save the world first,* he reminded himself. *Then you can worry about it.* "He's a really great guy, and his wife is supercool. You should try to get out to see him sometime."

"I'm going when I'm twenty." The age of consent, for werewolves. Eighteen was too damned young; everybody knew that. "I'm going to see if he needs a bodyguard, or maybe Lara will." The boy hugged himself and smiled. "I can't wait! I bet it's so cool, living in a mansion with all the boss weres."

"It's pretty great," Derik admitted. And it had been, until he'd fucked it up. Until he'd gotten the idea in his head that he could be a boss were. Dumb ass. "I'll put in a good word for you, if you want."

"Would you?" The boy's eyes, already big, went huge. "That'd be great. Thanks a lot."

"What do your folks think about your ambition?"

"Oh." The boy waved his parents away in the careless manner of preadolescents. "Mom wants me to stay out here and go to USC. Dad says I should aspire to more than being a 'spear carrier,' that's what he calls it. But I don't care. They're doing what *they* like. Now it's my turn. I mean, it will be."

"Well, while you're waiting to turn twenty, you could take a year or two of college, see if it suits you."

Terry shrugged.

"Terry! Get out of there and let the man have some privacy."

Terry sniffed the air. "Also, cookies are almost ready," he muttered.

"And cookies are almost ready! So get out here!"

Derik cracked up when the boy rolled his eyes and walked out, closing the door behind him. Jesus, had he ever been that young?

Sure he had; he and Michael and Moira had practically been littermates. Man, the shit they used to pull . . . it's a wonder Michael's mom hadn't drowned them all.

He picked up the phone and punched in the main number of the mansion.

"Wyndham residence," Jeannie answered, sounding harassed.

"Hey, Jeannie, it's me, D—"

"Lara! No! Don't you dare jump from there— don't you dare! Hello?"

"Uh, yeah, Jean, it's me, D—"

"Lara! I don't care if your dad does it all the time. Your dad's an idiot! And if you think I'm wasting my afternoon by driving you to the E.R.—hello?"

"It's Derik!" he hollered. "Can you patch me through to Antonia's house, please?"

"Jeez, stop with the yelling. Sure I will. How's it going? Save the world yet?"

"I'm gonna, just as soon as I finish my butter-scotch chip cookie," he said dryly.

"All righty. Patching you—Lara!—through now." There was a smooth, humming silence, then another ringing telephone.

"That *is* Morgan Le Fay," Antonia said by way of greeting. "She's an unspeakably evil creature and must be stopped from destroying the world. So get your ass back there and take care of her."

"What? Antonia? How'd you know it was—"

"I don't know about you," she said, "but I don't have a lot of time for dumb questions. Also, you're boring the tits right off of me."

"Come on, you should *see* this girl! There's no way she's the one. She's a goof, and she's *so* cute. Not to mention really clueless. I think you got your wires crossed, or whatever, on this one."

"Impossible. It's her. And you know what they say about the devil and pleasing faces. Now get back there and do your job."

"This sucks," he said to the empty line, and hung up.

"Cookie?" Marjie asked brightly when he stomped into the kitchen.

He took six.

SARA GUNN, THE UNSPEAKABLY EVIL CREATURE, NOticed the van as she was parking her loaner, but shrugged it off—Monterey wasn't *that* big a town, and lots of people went to and from the hospital. Monterey Bay General was a teaching hospital, the largest in two hundred miles, and the parking lot was the size of a small college campus.

She hurried through the main lobby, afraid to look at her watch to see how late she was. Dr. Cummings hated it when staff was late for grand rounds, though God knows he'd kept them waiting often enough. And even though she was *Dr. Gunn*, her doctorate was in nursing, so to old-school jerkoffs like Cummings, she was just a glorified maid with an extra diploma. Most days it slid off her like water off a duck, but days like today, when she knew she was in for a reaming and resented the hell out of it, she—

"Sara Gunn!"

She had been just about to step into the elevator when she heard her name and jerked her foot back. She turned, and her brain processed the half-dozen men dressed in—could it be?—flowing red robes. They had monks at the hospital now? Monks dressed in red? Like big lipsticks?

Armed monks?

An avid movie fan, Sara recognized nine-millimeter Beretta pistols when she saw them and was so startled, she froze in place. It was the context, of course. Sure. Seeing men in robes (big lipsticks!), toting guns, in the hospital, *her* hospital, was just . . . weird. If she had any sense, she'd be screaming her head off and hitting the floor, like several of the people around her, but she just stared, and now she was staring down the barrel of more than one pistol, and how many people could say *that* in life, that not only did they have one gun pointed at them, they had several, it was just too—

The one nearest her tripped on the newly mopped floor, knocking over the bright yellow CAUTION sign. He hit hard, too hard; she heard the wet snap as his neck broke.

She heard a muffled explosion from her left and flinched, but the pistol had misfired and the barrel imploded; the would-be gunman was screaming through a faceful of blood, screaming and staggering around and dripping. He'd lost all interest in her, and she could actually hear his blood pattering to the floor, which now needed to be mopped again.

The clip fell out of the third one's gun, something Sara had never seen before—a day for firsts! She didn't realize clips *could* fall out of guns, just slide out and clunk to the floor without anyone touching it, but this one had, and the robed man had taken to his heels, and then the lobby tipped crazily, as someone kicked her feet out from under her.

"Cross of Christ," Dr. Cummings grumped. He was lying on the floor beside her, and she realized he was the one who had knocked her down. His white beard, hair, and eyebrows were their usual chaotic mess; the eyebrows in particular resembled a pair of large, struggling, albino caterpillars. He looked like a pissed-off Colonel Sanders. "Leave the hospital for fifteen minutes, and the whole damned place falls apart. Last time I ever try to get coffee before rounds."

"Sorry I'm late," she said to the tile.

"Do you know why they're trying to kill you?"

"I have no idea. They—they knew my name." She realized she was existing in a ball of shock-induced calm. Well, that was all right. It was better than the screaming meemies. "But they're not having much luck, is the thing, and lucky for me."

She heard a terrific explosion, magnified in the lobby, and then heard it again, and saw the last two men fall, and saw the policeman standing by the Information Desk, gun out, very pale.

"Lucky for you," Dr. Cummings said, "there was a cop here."

"Uh-huh."

"Really lucky," he said, giving her a strange look.

"I'm going to go throw up now, I think."

"No you aren't. We're late for rounds." He seized her by the elbow—for a man in his late fifties, he was as strong as a PCP addict—and hauled her to her feet, then pushed her into the elevator. "You can puke later."

"I'll make a note of it in my Palm Pilot," she said, but already the urge was passing. Damn Dr. Cummings! Or bless him. She could never decide which.

7

THE POOL BOY WAS STILL THERE WHEN SHE GOT home. He was sitting on her front steps, chin cupped in hand, obviously waiting for her.

Sara brought the convertible to a smoking halt, bolted out the door, and ran to him. She had no idea why he was still there—Couldn't get a ride? Had news about her car?—and she didn't care. After the morning she'd had, she needed to talk to someone, and Dr. Cummings wasn't what you'd call a warm and nurturing person. This walking Ken doll would do just fine.

"You wouldn't believe it, you *wouldn't* believe it!" she cried as he stood. She seized a fistful of his shirt and shook it. He stared down at her. "A bunch of robed weirdos came to the hospital today and tried to kill me! There were guns all over the place!"

"I believe it," he said, nodding glumly.

"*And* I was late for grand rounds! And then I had to talk to the police for, like, ever. And I have no idea why you're here, but I have to tell you, I'm going in for a drink before I do anything, but you can have your car back, and maybe I'll have two drinks, I—I—oh, crap." She was fumbling with her keys and finally got her kitchen door unlocked.

Wordlessly, he followed her inside. She was momentarily uneasy, then dismissed it. Lightning wasn't going to strike twice today, and, besides, she knew this guy. Sort of. At least, her mechanic knew him. She was pretty sure.

"You wouldn't believe it, you wouldn't *believe* it," she babbled again, pawing through her freezer for the bottle of Grey Goose vodka. A screwdriver—light on the O.J.—was just what she needed. Possibly more than one. Possibly half a dozen. "What a crazy day! Even saying 'crazy day' doesn't do it justice—"

"Wait." At his command, she fell (uncharacteristically) silent. "You're Sara Gunn?"

"What? Of course I am. You know who I am. Yes. Am I out of ice? Oh, who cares. I'll drink it neat, if I have to . . . is vodka good with vanilla ice cream?"

"Sara Gunn of 6 Fairy Lane?"

"Yes. We've been *over* this." He was so beautiful, and so, so dumb. It wasn't fair. Like she needed *this*, today of all days. "Now, d'you want a drink? Because I'm having one. Or do you need a ride? Am I supposed to keep the blue one? It's a nice car and all, but not really my style. Although frankly, the day I've had, I don't give a shit either way." Belatedly, she remembered her manners. "I'll call the garage for you and have someone come pick you up. Okeydokey?"

He scowled at her, his gorgeous green eyes narrowing until they looked like pissed-off lasers. "D'you think you can ramp down the condescension a little bit, Miss Gunn? I get enough of that from my friend Moira."

"Doctor Gunn," she said automatically, even as she blushed. "Sorry," she added. "It's just that you seemed . . . confused. Even more than me.

And that's saying something." She reached for the phone. "I'll call the garage."

He took the phone out of her hand, moving so quickly she didn't realize he'd taken it, until she saw he was holding the cordless.

Odd. Odd! One second he'd been standing by the kitchen door, the next he was *right in front of her*. It was like watching a home movie, speeded up. Had she started drinking already?

He made a fist, still holding the phone, and then small pieces of plastic were raining down on her tile.

"I'm really, really sorry about this," he said dully. "It won't hurt. Just stand still."

"*What* won't hurt?"

His hands reached for her throat.

8

AT THE LAST SECOND, SHE WRIGGLED OUT OF HIS grip like a greased fish and kicked his shin pretty hard for a human. It actually hurt. "What is *wrong* with you?" she screeched. Her eyes were starry and wild. She reeked of tension and stress and fury. "Has everyone in this town gone completely nutso bonkers today?"

"Sort of." He took another swipe at her—if he could get his hands around her neck, he could end it in about half a second for her—she'd be in Heaven before she heard the snap. She ducked, and his hands closed on air. "It doesn't really matter. I'm so sorry. But I have to do this.

You're—I guess you're pretty dangerous. Sorry," he added lamely.

"Jerkoff, you have no idea! Now get the hell out of my house!" She snatched a statuette from the shelf by her head, and he ducked, but not fast enough—the five-inch-high Precious Moments figurine hit his forehead just above his right eye and exploded. By the time he shook the chips out of his hair and wiped the blood off his brow, she had darted down the hallway.

Grimly, he plodded after her. He didn't much like killing—heck, he'd only killed two people in his entire life, and they'd both been rogue were-wolves. That had been a totally different thing, not even in the same universe as what he was attempting now. He'd been defending the Pack then, and that was entirely different from snapping this poor girl's neck.

This is defending the Pack, too, buddy. You'd better believe it. Now get your head in the game!

He tried. He really did. He understood intellectually that this sort of thing went against his even-tempered grain. He also understood that this woman was a threat to his family, his entire way of life. Intellectually. But he wasn't angry at her, he wasn't scared of her, she wasn't fucking somebody dangerous, he wasn't defending territory, he wasn't feeling any of the things he needed to feel in order to be okay with breaking a person's neck.

Not to mention, Sara Gunn was a stone cutie. He really liked her, even on such short acquaintance. He liked her sass, he liked her scatterbrained good humor, and he *loved* the way she smelled: like roses wrapped in cotton. Since she was a doctor, he figured she was the comely female embodiment of the absentminded professor, which was cute all in itself. Another time and place, and he'd be tempted to charm her into getting a nice hotel room for the day and . . .

He caught up with her in the hallway, but she tripped as he reached for her neck, and he missed again. Well, of course he did. His heart was so completely not in this, it would have been funny if it wasn't so fucking depressing.

She kicked out at him from the floor and scrambled away. He reached again, and this time *he* tripped, falling hard enough to rattle his teeth.

Christ, will you get on? *Stop drawing this out! Bad enough you have to kill her, you've got to*

*play cat and mouse first? Scare her worse than
she is? Asshole.*

Except she wasn't so much scared as infuri-
ated. Oh, he could smell the fear, an undercurrent
beneath her rage, but she was primarily pissed.
He really liked her for it. Any other woman—
person!—would have been gibbering in the corner and begging for their life.

He climbed to his feet—only to be hit in the
face with a box of tampons. The white missiles
exploded out of the box and rained down on the
floor.

"Get . . . *lost*!" she shrieked, hurling a perfume bottle at him. This time he did duck, and
the bottle shattered behind him. Instantly the
hallway reeked of lavender, and he sneezed.

"Out!"

"I can't," he said, then sneezed again. "You
know, if you just stand still a minute, it'll be over
in—"

"Fuck you!"

"Right. Well, that's understandable. I mean, I
wouldn't stand still for this, either. It's okay," he
added soothingly, if inanely. What, exactly, was
okay? Nothing. Not a single goddamned thing.

He followed her into a bedroom and was momentarily startled at the sheer mess—it looked like someone had been killed in there. Then he realized that she was just a slob. There were clothes on almost every surface, and he couldn't tell what color the carpet was because of all the junk on the floor.

There were plenty of things to throw, too, and her aim was frightening—he was fast, but in her terror and anger, she was just a bit faster, raining missiles on him and shrieking like a fire alarm. He ducked about every two out of three, but that still left him vulnerable to: a jar of Noxema, an empty vase that smelled like stale water and dead flowers, a DVD case (*Vertigo*), a remote control, an empty box of Godiva chocolates, a box of computer discs, a hardcover copy of Stephen King's *The Stand*—cripes, how much did *that* weigh?

Have you noticed you haven't been able to kill her? Sure, you're phoning it in, but come on— you're a werewolf in your prime. So how come she's not a corpse?

His inner voice sounded weirdly like Michael, which made him inclined to ignore it. Normally.

But he realized—on the top of his mind this time, not just the bottom—that it was true. He hadn't been able to kill her. Every time he got close, she tripped, or he did, or she scored with another missile. His head was throbbing, and it was hard to think.

Still, she should have been toast about three minutes ago.

Okay, that was it. No more fooling around. She was treed on top of her dresser, which was bare of things to throw at the moment—she'd run out of ammo, finally. Instead of cowering, she crouched on it like a cat, one with several swipes left in its paws.

"You son of a bitch," she rasped, hoarse from all the screaming hysterics. "I haven't done a single thing to deserve this—"

"Well, not yet," he said.

"—and now look at this mess! Worse than usual! My house is a wreck, there's a tear in my skirt, there's dead bodies all over my workplace, and my crazy blond stud of a mechanic's helper is trying to kill me! Son of a bitch!"

"It's been a bad day for both of us," he admitted. Then, "Blond stud?" He was absurdly flattered.

"Fuck you! I want you to get lost and *leave me the hell alone!*"

She had screamed that last part, shrieked it, roared it. Her fury was intense, overwhelming—he couldn't get the smell of burning cedar out of his nose—it was practically choking him.

Suddenly, startlingly, the pain in his head intensified—cripes, it felt like his skull was splitting!—and he started to get dizzy for the first time in his life. It was extremely unpleasant. But before he could complain, or explain, everything got dark around the edges, and the room tilted, and then he didn't know anything, anything at all.

9.

MORE EXHILARATED THAN FRIGHTENED, SARA FIN-
ished taping Psycho Jerkoff to her kitchen chair
with her last roll of electrician's tape (a must for
any single woman's toolbox). Then she stood
back, looked at him for a long minute, and went
to get her bag.

She supposed she should find a phone and call
911, but she wasn't too worried about what's-
his-face getting out of that chair. In fact, she wondered if he'd ever get up again . . . he was the
color of kitchen plaster, and his body had a loose,
boneless feel she didn't like at all.

She found her bag, shook the dirt off it,
stepped over the spilled planter, and returned to

the kitchen. She briefly wished for a cell phone—she kept losing the fucking things, and she was paying for it now—and bent to Psycho Jerkoff. She peeled up one of his eyelids and grimaced—blown pupil. *Really* blown . . . the thing looked like a burst pumpkin, all brownish orange leaks. The sclera was shot with red threads, and his breathing was gasping, agonal.

What had she done to him? Was it like the rapist who was waiting—

But she wouldn't think about that now. What happened back then wasn't relevant to this poor fucker . . . he was dying before her eyes. He had tried to kill her, but that didn't mean she wanted him to go toes-up in her kitchen. Poor dumb ass. Even his eye was—

Actually, it looked a little better. Less red, and the pupil seemed to be . . . shrinking? Shrinking and pulling back, and the red was pulling back, too, disappearing, and then his perfectly whole pupil was *fixed on her,* and he shifted his weight, and she stumbled backward so fast she tripped over another chair and went sprawling.

10

"WELL," DERIK SAID, WAKING UP. "THAT WAS EMBAR-rassing."

She scuttled back from him, startled. He blinked down at her. What was she doing on the floor?

"What are you doing on the—"

"That was *fast*," she said, almost gasped. "One minute you were out cold, and the next—"

"I'm a quick healer." He started to get up, then realized he couldn't. He was—for crying out loud! "You've taped me," he observed. "Taped me to one of your kitchen chairs. That's a new one."

"Electrician's tape," she said, gesturing to the

depleted rolls on the counter. "A must for every household. Now go back to sleep so I can call the cops, you psychotic freak."

He wriggled. He could get loose, but it would take some time. She was fiendish in her cleverness! Tape was *tough*, and he sure couldn't untie it.

"You might not believe this," he said, "but I'm sort of glad." And he was! He hadn't been able to kill her. She was alive, and pissed, and he was actually kind of happy about it, and relieved. It was strange, and probably stupid, but right now he didn't care. "Sorry about the mess in your house."

"Oh, shut up. Listen, you were really screwed up. How, how did you get better?" she burst out. It was as if she'd been dying to ask the question. "You had a blown pupil—do you know what that means?"

"Well," he said, "it doesn't sound very nice."

"You got that right. It's indicative of an aneurysm, get it? Brain bleed? Nothing good, in other words. But you got better while I watched. Which is impossible."

"About as impossible as you still walking

around alive. And I told you, I'm a quick healer. Got anything to eat around here?"

"I'm supposed to feed you now? After you tried to kill me?"

"I'm hungry," he whined.

"Tell it to the judge." She reached for the phone, found it gone, then spotted the pieces of the handset all over the floor. "Damn it! I forgot about that. You're buying me a new phone, buster. And a new everything else we broke!" She knew, just *knew*, she would regret lending her bedroom phone to one of her former patients. Rose was a sweetie, but lending never meant lending, it always meant giving, and that was just—

"Sure, okay. Hey, listen, I've got to tell you something." Man oh man, Antonia would *not* be pleased. Neither would Michael. Fuck it. "I was sent on a mission to kill you."

"I gathered," she said dryly, "judging from all the murder attempts."

"No, I mean, my family sent me here. Specifically, to you. Because you're fated to destroy the world. And it's my job to stop you. Except I couldn't."

"And *you're* fated for a Thorazine drip, as soon as the nice men in the white coats come." But she looked troubled, as if she was hearing a voice in a distant room, one that agreed with him completely. "And I—I might have been wrong about your eyes. In fact, after the day I've had, a misdiagnosis wouldn't surprise me at all."

"Sure," he sneered back. "Because you make them *all* the time." This was a guess, but he figured Dr. Sara Gunn didn't get where she was by being a fuckup.

"Never mind. Now: What the hell did I do with my old phone?" she mused aloud, running her fingers through her red, red hair. It kept wanting to flop in her face, and she kept tossing it back with jerks of her head. It was the brightest thing in the room; he could hardly take his eyes off it. Off her. "Did I throw it out? I don't think I did . . . I never throw anything out, if I can help it . . . soon as you throw it out you need it again . . . stupid thing."

"Listen to me. I'm not crazy, though I totally understand why you think I might be."

"Do ya?" she asked with faux brightness.

"I couldn't kill you. Get it? Never mind that I

think my so-called sacred mission bites the bag; I was trying to kill you, and I couldn't do it. Don't you think that's a little bit weird?"

"No, I think *you're* a little bit weird." But she frowned.

"Hasn't stuff like this happened to you before? Weird days? Strangers popping up out of nowhere trying to do you harm? I can't believe my family's the only one who knows about you."

"This is California," she said, looking more than troubled; looking vaguely alarmed. "Weird stuff happens all the time out here. And it's not even an election year."

"Yeah, California, not the Twilight Zone." He wriggled more and the tape pulled at his arm hairs. "Ow!"

"Well, sit still."

"And starve to death? Forget it."

"Oh, for Pete's sake. How long have you gone without a meal?"

"Two hours."

"An eternity, I'm sure."

"Fast metabolism. Come on, you have to have *something* around here."

"Buddy, you have got some nerve." She

sounded almost . . . admiring? But she still looked pissed. Not that he could blame her. "Weird stuff . . . you probably said that because you were in on it."

"In on what?"

"Oh, like you don't know!"

"I *don't* know," he said patiently. "What are you talking about?"

"You don't know about the team of red-robed weirdos who tried to kill me at work." She said this with total skepticism.

"No, but I can't say I'm surprised. See, you're the bad guy."

"*I'm* the bad guy?"

"Yup. In fact, you're fated to destroy the world."

She touched her chest, looking flabbergasted. "*I* am?"

"Yup. That's why I was sent to make you take a dirt nap, so to speak. And I bet the crack team of weirdos was sent to do the same thing. So you should do three things: Feed me, untie me, and get the hell out of this house."

She stared at him.

"Don't think you have to do it in that order, either," he added, wriggling again. Fucking tape! Why couldn't she use plain old rope, like his ex-girlfriend?

"That's it," she finally said. "I'm calling the police. Right now." But she didn't move, and he could smell that she didn't mean it. She was too confused and curious.

"Okay, Morgan. Fetch the fuzz."

"What did you call me?"

"Morgan. It's your other name."

"I think I would know if I had another name."

"Obviously, you don't."

"Oh, piss off!" she snapped, which almost made him laugh. "I've had about enough of this 'mysterious stranger trying to kill me and then being all cryptic' garbage. Spit it out."

"Okay. You're the reincarnation of Morgan Le Fay."

She threw up her hands. "Oh, please! That's the best you could do?"

He shrugged, as much as he could mummified in tape as he was. "It's the truth. You're a bad witch, back to wreck the world. Sorry."

"First of all, Morgan Le Fay wasn't necessarily bad. Second—"

"How do you know that?"

"I did some papers on her in college. Second—"

"Uh-huh. Of all the people in the world, living and dead, you picked her. I bet your minor in college had something to do with her."

"Lots of people minor in European history. And as for picking Le Fay for a research topic— me and about a zillion other people through the ages," she said, but again looked vaguely troubled, as if listening to something he couldn't hear. Which with his hearing was impossible, frankly. "Tell me, the place where you live . . . are there a lot of doctors there? And little cups of pills?"

"Very funny, Morgan."

"Don't call me that," she said automatically, but with no real heat.

"Look, at least consider the possibility. I mean, why would I come here? I live in Massachusetts, for Christ's sake, but I come all the way across the country just to wreck *your* house?"

"That's the theory I was going with, yes," she admitted.

"Pretty shaky," he told her. "And today not only am I here, but another group of killers? Would-be killers, I mean? And what happened to them? How come you're not dead? You avoided me *and* them?"

"We haven't established that you're not one of them," she pointed out. "And they ran into some bad luck."

"Yeah, I'll bet. I'll bet that happens a lot around you."

"Well . . ." Her brow knitted, and she looked severely cute as she pondered. Her blue eyes narrowed and her forehead wrinkled. "I've always been lucky . . . but I don't think that proves anything."

"Since we're going to talk for a while—which I'm totally fine with, so don't sweat it—do you have an apple, or maybe you could fix me a PB&J, or something?"

"Again with the food! You've got a lot of nerve, anybody ever tell you that?"

"Pretty much every day, back home. So, do you?"

"I don't believe this," she muttered but, praise God, she turned to the counter, plucked an apple out of the bowl, grabbed a knife out of the rack, and rapidly cut the fruit into bite-sized pieces.

She stomped over to him and stuffed three chunks into his mouth.

"Fgggs," he said.

"You're welcome. So somebody sent you here to kill me because I'm the reincarnation of Morgan Le Fay, that's what you're telling me." He didn't answer because it wasn't an actual question. "And other people are also out to get me, because of this." He nodded, still chewing. "So I shouldn't call the cops, I should leave."

"With me," he said, swallowing.

"Oh, that's *rich*."

"I figure there's more to this than meets the eye, y'know? So we should take off and see if we can see what's what."

She was cutting up another apple in rapid, angry motions, and he eyed the knife a little nervously; if she got pissed enough to plant it in his eye, he'd probably never howl at the moon again. He was a fast healer, but there was some brain damage that couldn't be fixed, no matter how close the full moon was.

"See what's what," she repeated. "Yeah, sure. Let's get right on that." She jammed a few more pieces into his mouth and, although eating cut-up apples had never seemed particularly erotic to him before, the smell of her and the touch of her skin on his lips was starting to, um, cause him a little problem. Okay, a big problem.

He shifted in the chair and wished he could cross his legs. "Look, you get kind of weirded out whenever I suggest that there's maybe more to you than meets the eye," he said around a mouthful of apple. "So why don't you tell me? What happened before today? How come you're so lucky?"

"I don't *know*. I just am. I always have been. My mom used to call me her lucky break."

"Oh yeah? Where is she now?'

"She's dead."

"Oh. Sorry. Mine, too."

"Gosh, we've got all kinds of things in common," she said, rolling her eyes and shoving another chunk of apple between his lips.

"Meant to be, I guess," he said, chomping.

"Okay, so, I won the lottery. A couple of times," she said grudgingly.

"You *what*?" He knew she wasn't lying, but it was still surprising. "More than once?"

"I tend to get . . . windfalls . . . whenever I'm

short of money. And once I needed a few thousand to pay for the last quarter of school, and I won the lottery, and it was exactly the amount I needed. And I got a refund one year when I needed some extra money to—but everybody gets tax refunds."

"Yeah, but I've never even met one person who won the lottery, never mind won it twice."

"Four times," she muttered.

"Oh, for fuck's sake! And you're giving me shit like I'm crazy?"

"It doesn't mean anything," she insisted.

"Okay, Morgan—"

"Quit that!"

"—maybe you can explain how, at the exact moment you needed to get me out of the way, I get a freakin' *brain aneurysm*, how about that?"

"A happy coincidence?" she guessed.

"For Christ's sake."

"Actually," she said, clearing her throat, "there was a serial rapist in this area a couple years ago. And, um, he got in somehow while I was at school, but when I came home I found him dead in my kitchen."

"Brutally stabbed?"

"No, um, the autopsy showed he had a congenital heart defect, a minor one that shouldn't have given him any trouble, but for some reason, while he was waiting here to—to—well, he had an M.I. and died."

"What's an M.I.?"

"Myocardial infarction. Heart attack," she said impatiently.

He gaped at her. "Holy shit, I'm lucky to be alive!"

"Well, you really kind of are." She poked another piece of apple in his mouth. "Let the record show I still think you're nuts. Also, once when I overslept and missed the bus, it crashed, and half the people aboard were killed."

"Jesus Christ!" It was all he could say. This was worse—and cooler—than he had ever dreamed. "That's it, that's your magic. You're phenomenally fucking lucky. *All* the time."

"There's no such thing as magic." But that species of hellish doubt was on her face again. "Everybody's lucky."

"Sara, for God's sake. Listen to yourself."

"The team at the hospital . . ."

"Don't .tell me, let me guess. They were like the Three Stooges—or however many of them there were. Knocking heads, falling down, having heart attacks on the spot . . . and you walked away without a scratch."

"That might be true . . ."

"We should go clubbing some night."

She laughed unwillingly. "Sure we should. I'm sure the police will let you out in no time."

"Oh, come on! After all this, you're still calling the cops on me? We should get out of here!"

"You *did* try to kill me," she reminded him— like he needed it! He'd never live it down. Derik Gardner, badass werewolf, totally unable to kill a nurse. A nurse with a doctorate, but still. "And I've only got your word that you're not going to try again."

"Well, my word's good," he grumped. Of course, she couldn't *know* that. Not like another Pack member would know it. It made everything harder. Which was kind of cool. Yet aggravating. "And like I said, there's more to this than what we can smell. I think—"

"Than what we can *smell*?"

"Never mind. Look, let's do some digging, okay?"

"Okay!" she said with fake enthusiasm. "Do you want to be Nancy Drew or a Hardy Boy?"

He ignored the sarcasm . . . he'd had years of practice with Moira. "Let's find out what exactly you're supposed to do. I mean, you don't want to destroy the world, right?"

"This is the most surreal conversation I've ever had," she commented. "And no. Duh."

"So how come anybody who can see the future—I assume that's how the bad guys knew to come after you—says you're gonna do just that? Huh? Don't you think that's weird? Huh?"

"That's not the only thing I think is weird."

"Then hold on to your hat, sunshine."

She eyed him warily. "What? I'm not really up to more surreal revelations . . ."

"I'm a werewolf."

"Damn it! What did I just *say*?"

11

"I'M A WEREWOLF," THE GORGEOUS NUT JOB SAID
again. He shifted in the chair and winced. She
suspected he was sore . . . certainly there was
plenty of dried blood on his forehead and speck-
led all over his shirt. She felt sorry for him and
stomped on the emotion. "Soon to be a hairless
one, but there you go."

"Whine much? Try getting a bikini wax."

"I'll pass."

"Look, one thing at a time, all right?" Sara
tried not to show how rattled she was. She suspected she was fighting a losing battle. As if her
day hadn't been upsetting enough, she was actually turned on by hand-feeding Hunka Hunka

Burning Looney. She could feel the stubble on his chin when she popped more apple slices into his mouth, could feel the warmth of his face, smell the apple sweetness of his breath, could

(I could do anything to him, anything at all.)

feel his . . . his . . .

(He couldn't stop me. He's tied up. I could sit on his lap and do . . . do anything . . .)

Aw, nuts. His lips were moving. More nonsense about

(the true you)

Morgan Le Fay, no doubt.

"What?" she asked.

"I *said*, one of my Pack members told me what you were going to do, and my—my boss, I guess you'd call him, he sent me here to take care of you. And not in a good way, F.Y.I."

"Sounds like a real prince," she muttered, trying not to stare at his mouth.

Derik shrugged. "More like a king, actually, and he's okay. He's my best friend, so I had to leave before I killed him."

"Oh yeah?"

"Yeah. I mean, I couldn't imagine anything worse than killing a friend."

"That's pretty bad," she admitted, wondering when she'd checked her sanity at the door. This was definitely the most surreal conversation she'd had in . . . ever. "It's probably just as well you left town to kill me instead."

"To try to kill you," he corrected. Then he grinned, showing many teeth. It was so startling—a white flash, and cripes, those chompers looked *sharp*—that she nearly took a step back. "And I like you, too, by the way," he added, which made no sense, but who cared? "You are, in case nobody's told you, extremely cute. Are you a natural redhead? You are, aren't you?"

"Never mind," she said severely. "I'm going in the back room now, to call the police. You're extremely confused, if gorgeous, and I . . . have had . . . enough."

"Oh, me, too," he assured her. "I don't think I've been less comfortable in my life. So if you don't mind . . . and even if you do . . ." Then he did something like an all-over shrug, and she heard tearing tape, and then he—he was standing up!

One more time: He was standing up!

"Gah," she said, or something like it. How

had he—how had he torn through all that—and the arm of the chair was broken, too, which was weird, and—

He was grabbing her! Well, reaching for her. Taking her by the arms

"Gah!"

and pulling her into a snug embrace

"Gah!"

and bending his head toward hers

"Ga—mmph!"

and then his mouth was on hers, moving deliciously across hers, and she was grabbing his shoulders to, um, push him away, okay, she was going with that, yeah, pushing him away, except now she was up on her tiptoes, the better to fit against him, and he smelled delicious, he smelled like the woods in springtime, and his mouth, oh God, his mouth was warm, and his breath was redolent of apples and . . . and . . .

He'd broken the kiss and was standing three feet away from her. She'd never seen him move. She'd blinked, and he was done. Her mind tried to process his speed and couldn't do it. Just . . . couldn't.

"Sorry," he said cheerfully. "Wanted to do *that*

for oh, about the last four hours. Now it's out of my system. Okay, maybe not. So! What's next, sunshine?"

"Gah?" she asked, raising a trembling hand to her mouth.

"I think we should put our, um, heads together and figure out what's what."

"You're *not* a werewolf," she said, because it was the only thing she could think of.

He sighed and walked into her living room, squatted, picked up her couch, stood, and held it in one hand, in much the same way she would hold a tray. Fortunately, she had vaulted ceilings.

"You're not gonna make me juggle it, are you?" He tossed her couch a foot in the air, caught it, tossed it again. "I don't think I have enough room."

"So you work out," she said through numb lips. "That doesn't mean you—you—you know."

"Get fuzzy and bark at the moon one night a month?"

"Well . . ."

"Look, I believed *you're* a hideously danger-ous sorceress fated to destroy the world."

"Don't do me any favors," she snapped. "And put that thing down."

"Say it," he sang. He wasn't even out of breath!

"Just put it down, and we'll talk some more, okay?"

"Saaaaaaaay it . . ."

"Fine, fine! You're a werewolf, and I'm a demented sorceress. Now let go of my couch," she begged.

"Okay." He carefully put it back where he'd found it. "So, now what?"

"Well, I'm not going to destroy the world, I'll tell you that right now." She crossed her arms in front of her chest. It was easier to be brave—sound brave, anyway—when he was all the way across the room.

"Works for me. How about another kiss? No? Spoilsport."

"You're really weird," she informed him.

"That's what they tell me." He was weirdly cheerful. He was, in fact, the smilingest guy she'd ever known. Maybe he was mildly retarded.

" 'They' being . . . ?"

"My Pack."

"Your pack."

"Uppercase *P*."

"Mmm. Of werewolves, right?"

"Yup."

"Who sent you out here to stop me from destroying the world."

"Yup."

"But you're not going to kill me."

"Well . . ." He spread his hands apologetically. "I couldn't, first of all. I mean, really couldn't. I felt bad about it, but I was gonna do it, don't get me wrong. But . . . I didn't. And in case no one's ever told you, an aneurysm hurts like a bastard."

"Thanks for the tip."

"So I figure, we team up, figure out who the *real* bad guys are, and save the world."

"But what if *you're* the real bad guy?"

"Well, I know it's not me. And you were pretty upset about something when you showed up. I'm betting you've met the real bad guys. So, I'll help you get 'em."

"Why?" she asked suspiciously.

"Well. It'll help me both personally and professionally, see, because I've kinda wanted to be on my own, and I figure this is the chance to show what I can do. Just . . . don't blow up the planet in the meantime, okay? I'd never live it down. I mean—how totally embarrassing."

"Team up?" Why was the idea as exciting as it was frightening? "Like that, eh?"

He smiled at her and, oddly, the expression wasn't startling. Maybe because he wasn't showing so many teeth. "Like that. So, what do you say?"

"I say we're both nuts." She pressed the heel of her hand to her forehead. "I can't believe I'm considering this. I can't believe I'm *not* calling the police. I can't believe . . ."

"What?"

"Never mind."

"Oh, that? Don't worry about *that*. I told you, I like you, too."

"Swell," she muttered.

12

"I WISH YOU WOULDN'T DO THAT."

"Sorry." He pulled back so his head was inside the car. "Can't help it. This place smells *great*."

"Look, it's weird enough that you stick your head out of the car like a big—well, you know. But do you have to do it while you're driving?"

"No," he sulked.

"Take a left at the light."

He did, and Monterey Bay General loomed before them. Sara stared at the brick building. It was completely perfect that they should show up here first. MB General had been her home forever. She'd learned there, worked there, fallen in love there, worked there, got dumped there, slept there, worked there, been forged there, worked there, found out she was an orphan there, grown up there.

Found a father there.

Well, at least Derik hadn't tried to kill her. Again.

"I forgot," she said abruptly. "What's your last name?"

"Gardner."

"Oh." That sounded almost . . . normal. Safe and normal. "Okay. So, I guess you already know my name."

"Yup."

"Of course," she muttered. Stupid! He'd only told her the whole silly story, and more than once. Maybe she couldn't retain the facts because she couldn't swallow them. Frankly, she still wasn't sure if she was buying into this whole "you're doomed to destroy the world" thing, but at the very least, it was more interesting than hanging out in her mechanic's garage.

"You okay?" he asked. "You look like you're about to jump out of the car." He parked. "Which you totally shouldn't do. I mean, you guys are mega-fragile. I don't know how you walk around in those breakable bodies of yours."

"You kind of get in the habit of it, if you're born in one of those bodies."

"Poor thing." He shook his head.

"Never mind."

"OKAY," SHE SAID NERVOUSLY. "WE'RE GONNA GO find Dr. Cummings. He's kind of like my mentor. He and my mom were good friends, and he took care of me after she—after she died. He knew a lot of stuff about my family that he would never talk about, and he—he's always been good in a crisis." More like completely unruffled, all the time. And hadn't he recovered awfully quickly from the morning attack? He'd been more annoyed than scared . . . not a typical reaction. Except from him. But it was enough to make her wonder. "Anyway, we'll find him and see what he has to say, and maybe figure out where to go from there. Okay? Is that okay?"

"You're the killer sorceress," he said easily. "I guess we'll go wherever you say."

"Knock that off, or no Milk Bones for you tonight."

He groaned, which caused several female heads to swivel in their direction. Derik was slightly larger than life . . . hell, he was slightly larger than his T-shirt, which bulged and rippled in interesting directions. He was by far the largest man in the hospital lobby. Possibly in the hospital. Or the city. "Don't start with the dog jokes, okay?"

"That depends on you," she said smugly. "Now come on. Dr. Cummings is probably in his office."

"What's he look like?"

"Like an angry Colonel Sanders."

Derik snorted. "Does he have white hair and a white beard? And does he eat tons of Corn Nuts?"

She stared at him and almost didn't get into the elevator. Sheer momentum carried her to his side. "Have you been following me?"

He looked at her curiously. "That's gonna make you mad? That's worse than trying to kill you?"

"People have tried that before. I'm almost

used to it. But I fucking *hate* being followed," she snapped. "It's sneaky and dishonest and nasty."

"Take it easy!" He threw his hands in the air. "Seriously, Sara, don't get mad, okay? Just caaalm down. I wasn't following you. I can smell this Dr. Cummings guy on you, that's all."

"That's *all*?" She stabbed the button for the fifth floor. Derik's slight panic was sort of amusing. It was nice to have the upper hand with someone so good-looking. And she knew, she just *knew*, he was one of Those Guys. Every woman in the lobby had been staring at him, and he hadn't even noticed. One of Those Guys never had a clue how great-looking they were. It was annoying. No, it was nice. No, it was annoying.

"He must have hugged you or grabbed you or something. There's a couple of white hairs on your left shoulder. I mean, you got a nose like mine, you don't have to follow anybody. So mellow out, okay?"

"Dr. Cummings knocked me down in the lobby," she admitted. "He was kind of pissed."

Derik frowned. "At you?"

"No, about the killers making us late for grand rounds."

"Seriously?"

"Yes."

"Huh. Yeah, we better go talk to this guy. Shit, maybe we can recruit him."

"I'm sure," she said dryly, walking the Gauntlet—what everyone called the fifth floor physicians' offices—while Derik fell into step beside her, "that he'd be thrilled."

She stopped outside Cummings's office and raised a hand to knock.

"That door says Dr. Michaels," Derik pointed out.

"Mmm. It's one of the many ways Dr. Cummings tries to ensure interns don't bug him."

She rapped twice.

"Go away, or I'll have you fired!"

"That's another one," she explained, and opened the door.

"Oh, wonderful, it's Dr. Nurse Gunn. Or is it Nurse Gunn, Doctor? Don't let the door crush your tiny head on the way out."

"This man here," Sara said, indicating Derik, who was openly fascinated by Dr. Cummings's fuzzy eyebrows, "tells me I'm Morgan Le Fay."

Dr. Cummings grunted and started pawing through the pile of last year's *Lancet*.

"And that he was sent to kill me so I wouldn't destroy the world."

Dr. Cummings found the issue he wanted and settled back in his chair. He grunted again, an invitation for Sara to keep speaking.

"And I was wondering," she continued, feeling foolish, "what you might have to say about that."

"I'm surprised the boy's still alive," Dr. Cummings said, not looking up from the magazine. "And disappointed, I might add. I don't have anything to say beyond that, Your Highness."

She blinked. Thought that over. Started to speak. Changed her mind. Changed her mind again. Said: "Your Highness?"

"Well. You *are* the sister of a king. A centuries-dead king, but there you go."

"Oh, dude," Derik said, and flopped down into the nearest chair. "You're in major trouble, Cummings."

"You keep your hands to yourself, werewolf."

Sara's mouth fell open. Derik nearly fell out of

the chair. "Dude! How'd you know? You are so *not* Pack."

"Do I look like I like my steak served *tartare*?" Cummings snapped. "It's all over you. Predators walk, stand, move, and run quite a bit differently from the rest of us. If you want to fool Homo sapiens, I'd advise not walking around sizing everyone up like you're wondering how they'd taste. And as for *you*, Your Highness," he said, swiveling toward Sara, "what are you doing with this—this riffraff? Fooled by his over-the-top handsomeness, I've no doubt. Strongly consider killing him, dear. Werewolves are nothing but trouble, and they do *not* make good husbands."

"That's not true!" Derik said hotly.

"Where's your father, lycanthrope?" Dr. Cummings asked with deceptive courtesy.

"He's . . . um . . . look, let's stay on-topic, shall we? And don't call me that. Cough up what you know, chum. Right now." He turned to Sara, who was desperately trying to follow the conversation. "But let's get back to this for a sec—we do *too* make good husbands. You know—once we find the right girl."

Dr. Cummings made a sound. It was not a sound of encouragement.

"See, most of the guys I know really want a mate—a wife, I mean—and kids. They really do. But there aren't very many of us, and there's tons and tons of *you* guys, so lots of times they don't really think it through before they settle down, and, well, humans are different from Pack, it's nothing to be embarrassed about—"

"Derik." She was exasperated—who *cared?*—and amused at his distress. "Can we stay focused on this whole Your Highness thing? And you!" Dr. Cummings flinched as she shook a finger at him. "Start talking. Start with, 'I moved to Monterey Bay and knew your mother before you were born,' and end with, 'and then you and a werewolf came to my office.' Start *now*."

"Yeah!" Derik added.

"Don't raise your voice to me, pup." Cummings looked at Sara. "I moved to Monterey Bay because by my art I knew Morgan Le Fay was to be born there in seventy-two hours. I found you at this hospital and befriended your mother. I explained to your mother who you were, but she wouldn't believe me, and forbade me to tell you.

I kept you safe these many years and looked after you after your mother died. Now Arthur's Chosen is trying to kill you. It has nothing to do with saving the world. They just don't like you. Then you and a werewolf came to my office." He picked up his magazine again.

"Oh, dude." Derik rubbed his forehead. "You are so asking for a heart attack or for your lungs to pop or your eyeballs to explode or something. I mean, I don't even *know* her and that whole story pissed me right off."

"My mother?" Sara coughed and tried again. "My mother knew this?"

"No. You weren't listening, Dr. Gunn, a trait I've discussed with you before."

"Sorry," she muttered.

"Want me to pull his lungs out for you?" Derik asked brightly.

"Try it, lycanthrope."

"I told you not to call me that."

"You guys, cut it *out*!" she snapped. "Finish what you were saying, Doctor."

He sniffed. "Well. As earlier, I said your mother refused to believe the truth. And she did. She willfully would not let herself believe. She went to her grave thinking you were like every other kid. She was, in fact, determined you were like every other kid. No matter what she saw. No matter what you did." Dr. Cummings paused. "A nice woman," he said at last, "but not terribly bright."

"Do *not* talk about Sara's dam like that," Derik growled.

"It's a free country, whelp, and do I look like I'm worried about irritating someone who licks his testicles during a full moon?"

Derik's eyes bulged, and Sara choked back a laugh. She knew at once that the big blond stud was not used to humans in their fifties dishing out shit.

"Okay, okay," she said, holding her hands up. "Let's stay focused."

"I do *not* lick my—"

"So, Dr. Cummings, why you? Why have you been sticking so close?"

"To protect you from the occasional moron who wants to kill you because of who you are." He glanced meaningfully at Derik, whose hands were clenching and relaxing, clenching and relaxing. "Or, rather, who you were."

"And those guys this morning?"

"I told you. Arthur's Chosen."

A long silence and, when it appeared Dr. Cummings had nothing more to say, Sara said, exasperated, "And who are they?"

"Buncha losers, probably," Derik muttered. "Out to get you just because they can."

"And *your* purpose in our fair town was what, exactly?" Dr. Cummings asked sharply. "I'm sure I can guess. Your alpha gave you your marching orders, and off you went, without a question or a murmur. Typical Pack behavior."

"He did not! I mean, I decided to come on my own. Well, um, and what the hell do you know about it, Cummings?"

Dr. Cummings shrugged, and began rooting around for a pack of cigarettes. Smoking was, of course, forbidden in the hospital. Only Dr. Cummings dared to try. "I spent some time—years— in the company of a lady lycanthrope. She'd been banished from your Pack for some trivial reason, and was lonely."

"Where is she now?" Sara asked, interested in spite of herself. She'd never seen Dr. Cummings in the company of anyone but her mother. In fact, there were rumors that he was gay.

"A new Pack leader came to power, forgave her for her unbelievably minor transgression, and off she went, back to the Cape to live happily catching rabbits with her teeth."

"Who was it?" Derik asked. "I probably know her family."

"Never you mind. My point is, I wouldn't start pointing fingers at Arthur's Chosen, because your own reasons for being here aren't exactly beyond reproach."

"Uh-huh! I'm trying to save the world, pal. Grief from puffing human busybodies I so *don't* need."

"Arthur's Chosen," Sara said, again trying to bring them back on track. "What's their story?"

Cummings shrugged and lit a cigarette. "Rabid followers of the King Arthur legend. You know, of course, that Arthur was betrayed by his half sister, Morgan Le Fay, and it's ultimately why he fell in battle. Arthur's Chosen think that if they get rid of *you*, Arthur will finally return."

"So," Derik said, "they're cracked in the head."

"Well, yes. They're fanatics. A tough group to reason with."

"Just a minute," Sara said. "Morgan's supposed 'evil nature' is legend, not fact. In fact, a lot of people believe today that Morgan's wickedness was the invention of misogynist monks."

Both Dr. Cummings and Derik shrugged. Sara resisted the urge to throw up her hands. Men! God forbid they look at history in a woman-friendly fashion. Morgan Le Fay was probably a perfectly nice woman for her time. Strong-willed, sure. But wicked and evil and a dark sorceress? Feh.

"But how do they know Sara's Morgan?"

"The same way I did. The stars, old books, legends, prophecies. How did *you* know?"

"One of my Pack members can see the future," Derik admitted. "She said if I didn't get my butt to Sara's address pronto, the world was gonna blow up, or whatever."

"Hmm. Charming. So, what are your plans?"

Derik looked blank. Sara said, "Plans?"

"To eliminate the threat to your personal safety, to not destroy the world—the prophecies all agree on *that*, I'm sorry to say—you know. Your plans."

"Uh . . ."

"Great," Dr. Cummings grumped. "I swear, Sara, you get dumber every year."

"Watch it," Derik warned.

"And you, I suspect, were never the sharpest knife in the drawer."

"Dude, I am *so* going to make you eat your ears."

Dr. Cumming sighed. "Very well. Arthur's sect has its home base in Salem, Massachusetts. Go there. Smite your enemies. Have a hot fudge sundae. The end."

"Wait, wait, wait. If you knew all this was going to happen, why didn't you warn me? Why didn't you tell me about Arthur's Sect ten years ago?"

"Right. I see now that I have failed you. Because you certainly would have believed me and left at once for Salem."

"Might have," she mumbled.

"Don't you see, Sara? I had to wait until forces started moving in on you. It's the only way there would have been a chance of you believing me.

The sect would never have harmed you as an infant, because all the prophecies say you don't destroy the world until you're fully grown."

"Wait, wait," Derik protested. "So why not kill her when she was a baby? Save the world that way?"

"Because the sect can't use her if she's dead, stupid mongrel. And she's not so easy to kill, in case you forgot. Which wouldn't surprise me."

"But how do they use her to destroy the world? These Arthur guys?"

Dr. Cummings shrugged. "No one knows. Only that she is integral to the plot. Kill her as an infant, and who knows what will happen? Wait until she's fully-grown—very fully grown, Sara, time to lay off the bagels—and risk the world being destroyed. It's not an easy choice. Most of us decided to watch and wait. Now go away."

"It's not nice to kill old guys," Derik muttered under his breath. "It's not nice to kill old guys. It's not nice to—"

"All I could do was stick close, which I have, and now I'm done, and it's Miller time." Dr. Cummings clapped his hands sharply, making

Sara and Derik jump. "Now go! Off to Salem. Good-bye."

Derik and Sara looked at each other, then shrugged in unison. "I'm game if you are," she said. "I don't want to walk into the hospital again and worry about Arthur's Chosen hurting bystanders."

"I'm going where you go."

"How touching," Dr. Cummings said. "I've approved your vacation request as of thirty seconds ago. I suggest you don't delay."

"Why?" Sara asked. "Is there something you're not telling us?"

"No, I'm just bored now. Good-bye."

"What a sweetheart," Derik muttered once they were on the other side of the door.

"Off to Massachusetts," Sara said, "dodging killers along the way, and with a werewolf bodyguard."

"Don't forget about the hot fudge sundaes."

13

"WE CAN'T GO BACK TO YOUR PLACE."

"Agreed. Besides, it would take about six hours of cleaning before the house was livable again. Thanks again, by the way."

Derik ignored her sarcasm. "And I sure can't show up at the mansion with *you*."

"Uh-huh. Err . . . why is that, again?"

"Because I was supposed to kill you, duh."

"Don't say duh to me," she ordered. "I get enough of that from Dr. Cummings."

"Yeah, cripes, what a grouch. Guy's not afraid of anything, is he?" Derik said this in a tone of grudging admiration. "But anyway, about you— I can hardly walk through the front door and say, 'hey, guys, here's Morgan Le Fay, didn't feel like killing her, what's for lunch?' "

Sara frowned. "So you're saying you're going to get into trouble for this?"

Derik stretched, wiggling in the driver's seat, then pulled into a convenience store parking lot. "Maybe. Kind of. Okay, yes."

"Derik, you can't—I mean, I appreciate you giving up your sacred holy mission of premeditated murder and all, but don't your kind banish Pack members for, like, teeny tiny reasons? Never mind huge reasons like not fulfilling your mission?"

"We have a group mentality," he explained. "So if you do something that hurts the group, or may possibly hurt the group, it's bye-bye time."

"So you—you can't go back?" Sara tried not to sound as horrified as she felt. She was lonely—well, alone—by circumstance. Her father had died the day she was born; her mother when she was a teenager. But Derik was deliberately giving up his family . . . for her. It was touching. And cracked. "Not ever?"

He yawned, apparently unconcerned. "Well, I figure it's like this: Either you destroy the world, in which case, my alpha can't kick my ass, or you don't, in which case, my alpha will know I was right. Kind of a win/win for me."

"Except for the possible death of billions."

"Well, yeah. There's that."

"But you can never see your friends again?" Sara was having trouble letting this go. "Your family?"

"I was going to leave anyway. It was either that, or—anyway, I had to go."

"Well, thanks," she said doubtfully. "I—thanks. What are we doing here?"

"I'm starved."

"Again?"

"Hey, we don't all weigh a hundred pounds and have the metabolism of a fat monkey."

"Oh, very nice!" she snapped. "Well, as long as you're here, let me get my cash card, I'll grab some money."

His hand closed over hers, which was startling, to say the least. He was very warm. His hand dwarfed hers and, in the California sunlight, the hair on the back of his knuckles was reddish blond. She was fascinated to note that his index finger was exactly as long as his middle finger. "Nope."

She stared into his green, green eyes. "What, nope?"

"We're on the way to Salem, right? Chances are, there's gonna be some bad guys on our tail. Right?"

"What, you're asking me? Ten hours ago my biggest problem was finding a pair of panty hose that didn't have a run in them."

"*So*, you can't leave a money trail," he continued patiently. "No cash cards, no credit cards. And if you make a big bank withdrawal, my Pack's gonna know you're alive. They'll assume I'm dead, and then there's gonna be real trouble."

"How would they even know—never mind, don't tell me. We can't go across the country with no money," she pointed out.

"Yeah, yeah. I'm working on that one."

"What a relief," she said, getting out of the car and following him up the sidewalk. "Seriously. You have no idea."

"Aw, stick a sock in it. You—watch it." He grabbed her elbow and pulled her out of the way just as a teenager came barreling through the door of the store. The kid stopped for a minute, utterly panicked, and they all heard the wail of sirens at the same time.

Well, probably not, Sara thought. Probably

Derik heard them about a minute earlier. Aggravating man. And what happened when the moon rose? What *then*? Did she really believe he was going to turn into a wolf and run around peeing on fire hydrants?

"Shit!" the teen cried, and started to dart around them. Derik stepped in his way—

"Don't do that," Sara said sharply. "He might have a gun."

"He *does* have a gun," Derik replied, bored.

—and the teen suddenly thrust a paper bag at Sara, who tightened her grip around it purely by reflex.

They both watched the kid race out of the parking lot.

Sara opened the sack, which was bulging with twenties, tens, and fives. "Oh," she said. "Well. Um. I seem to have come into some untraceable cash for our trip."

Derik slapped the heel of his hand to his forehead, then shoved Sara back toward the car. "Let's get out of here before the cops come." He jumped into the convertible, fighting a grin. "You lucky bitch."

*   *   *

"SO, WE NEED ANOTHER CAR."

"Okay," Sara said. They had left the Monterey city limits, and she had just finished counting the money. Eight hundred sixty-two dollars even. No change. "Um, why?"

"Because my Pack rented this one for me. They can track it. We have to leave it and find something on our own."

"Okay."

"So, do it."

"Do *what*?"

"You know. Work your hocus-pocus and wish us up a car."

"It doesn't work like that."

"The hell it doesn't."

"I don't have conscious control over it," she explained, trying—and failing—to smooth her hair out of her face. Convertibles were sexy and cool in the movies, but in real life you couldn't see for all the hair flying around. And she dreaded trying to pull a brush through the mess when they parked. Not that she had a brush. But still. "Heck, until you showed up, I didn't think I could do anything special at all. Except bowl," she added thoughtfully. "I'm great at that."

"Yeah, I bet those pins just happen to fall over for you all the time. Concentrate," he ordered. "We need . . . an untraceable . . . car."

"Stop . . . talking . . . like that."

He slapped the steering wheel with his palm. "Shit. Well, I guess I could steal one . . . except we'd have to do that at least every day or so."

"Why aren't we taking a plane? Isn't it a four- or five-day drive?"

"You want to show airport security your ID? Because I don't think that's, y'know, too cool. Which also lets out renting a car, and taking a train."

"Are there that many werewolves running around the country?"

"No. There's only about three hundred thousand of us, worldwide. But still. I think it's too important to take chances. I'd hate to fuck this up through bad luck, y' know? Not that you exactly have bad luck. But still. I'm not crazy about taking chances. Okay, I am, but not chances of this magnitude. Get it?"

"Hardly. And you can't ask any of your—um, your family—the Pack, or whatever you call it—for a car?"

"Well, I could, but I'd rather not take a chance on anything getting back to Michael—my alpha," he explained. "I'd risk spending a night or two with local Pack members, because my mission is top secret—"

"Excellent, Mr. Bond."

"*Anyway*, most of the Pack doesn't know what I'm up to. Just the East Coasters. So it's no big deal to show up on someone's doorstep and crash for the night. But to do that, and be in a situation where I'd have to borrow a car, and have you in tow . . . that might get back to the wrong set of ears."

"So, what?"

"So, we need a car. We'll drive for a while, then crash."

"I'll tell you right now," Sara declared, "no more convertibles!"

"Aw, how come?" he whined. "How can you not like the wind in your face?"

She pointed to her head, which, thanks to mussed curls, was almost twice as large as usual. "Forget it, Derik. For-get-it."

"Aw, you look cute."

"And you're deranged, but we established that a couple hours earlier. *No* convertibles."

"Well, I'm not driving a zillion miles—"

"Three thousand, five hundred," she said dryly.

"—locked up in a steel box, I can tell you that right now, Sare-Bear!"

"Ew, don't call me that. Sare-Bear? Ugh."

" 'Cuz you look like a cute little bear with your hair all over the—"

"Stop talking. What? You're claustrophobic?"

"No. I just don't like being shut up in a steel box for hours and hours a day."

"So, you *are* claustrophobic."

"No, it's just . . . that fake carpet . . . the upholstery . . ." He shuddered. "It reeks, man. It totally reeks."

"You know what we need?"

"For you not to destroy the world?"

"Besides that. We need a truck. A nice big truck with four-wheel drive and a supercab."

"What's a supercab?"

"It's a truck that seats two or three people in the front seat and a couple in the backseat. There's plenty of space to store our stuff, and if you start feeling like the upholstery is closing in on you, you can ride in the back while I drive. Your hair mussed in the breeze, your ears flopping behind you . . . it'll be great."

"Can you destroy the world right now?" he asked. "Because if I gotta put up with one more dog joke . . ."

"And if we don't get a motel room or don't want to stop for long, we can spread some sleeping bags out in the back and sack out there. We'd have to stop and use some of this cash to buy camping equipment, but that'd be easy enough."

He frowned at her. He blinked at her. At last he said, "That's kind of brilliant."

"Well," she said modestly, "I *am* a doctor."

"Okay, so. We try to steal a truck."

"And what are we going to do when we catch up with Arthur's Chosen?"

"Let's get there first," he said grimly, and she had no reply to that.

14

"THIS IS INSANE," SHE COMMENTED.

"It is not. Now try to look like we're not stealing a car."

"But we *are* stealing a car."

"Will you cut that out? Look casual. Lean on the door."

"The one you're trying to open?"

Derik resisted the urge to strangle Sara. This was an interesting improvement over resisting the urge to kiss her. You'd think, since he'd saved her life—well, sort of, in that he hadn't tried to kill her again—and because he was helping her hunt down Arthur's Big Fat Losers, that she'd be a little grateful. Or at least nicer. But nooo. It was blah-blah-blah and bitch-bitch-bitch. Like she could do any better than a full-grown werewolf! Okay, well, maybe she could. But that was irrelevant. Wasn't it?

"It's just that this is an extremely insane idea," she was explaining, like he'd gone retarded.

He grabbed the door handle again and tried to smell her hair without her catching on. Roses and cotton—yum! And how cute did she look in the convertible with those red curls flying all over the place? Her nose was sunburned now, and he even liked the shade of pink.

She turned to give him a suspicious look, and he held his breath in mid-sniff. Then, to distract her, he said, "Show me another place that has all the cars lined up, with their keys in the ignition." He spread his arms to indicate the Enterprise Car Rental lot. "Huh? Show me. That's all I ask."

"Show *me* another place that has *less* paperwork on any one of these cars. You don't think they do a head count or whatever—a grille count—before the last guy goes home for the day? They'll know it's gone in a cold minute."

"So we find another car rental place," he said, "and steal from there."

"Help you folks?"

They both spun, Derik swearing under his breath. Sure, the guy had snuck up on him from upwind, and sure, Sara was sort of distracting—she kind of jammed his radar, so to speak—but that was no excuse. No fucking excuse!

"We were just looking," Sara explained, after clearing her throat and trying a smile.

The fella who'd hailed them looked more nervous than they did—and more angry than Derik felt. His gray suit was rumpled, and his tie was flying over his shoulder in the breeze. His brown hair was wisping about, and his watery blue eyes were alternately starey and darting. Derik started to grab Sara's shoulder to pull her behind him when he got a whiff of burning silk—the smell of desperation.

"Uh-oh," he muttered.

"You folks need a car? I'll tell you what. You can have that truck right over there." He pointed to a shiny, brand-new, red pickup truck, complete with supercab and about fourteen antennas.

They looked at the truck, glowing at them almost like a mirage, or the Holy Grail—Derik expected to hear a choir of angels humming—then looked at the sales guy.

"I've had it with this place," he muttered. "Promote *Jim Danielson* over me? The guy comes in an hour late every day and leaves an hour early. And don't get me started on his lunch breaks. They're more like miniature leaves of absence. The guy's fucking the manager's daughter so *he* gets the promotion? *Him?*"

"We, uh, don't want you to get in any trouble," Sara said.

"And we don't want you to get any closer," Derik warned.

"No, look, it's okay, see?" The frustrated Enterprise employee grinned, which looked fairly ghastly. "You guys know how to drive a standard transmission, right?"

"Driving a stick is so *not* the big problem in this scenario," Derik said.

"Shhh!" Sara's elbow jabbed him in the side. "Let him finish."

"It's no problem. I'll just fix it in the computer. Nobody will even know about it. Go on, take it. You can help me stick it to my boss." He stared off at the horizon for a moment, looking haunted. "I just—not today. I put up with it, and I put up with it, but for some reason, today I just—I can't do it. Not one more day. So go on."

"STOP LOOKING SO DAMNED SMUG," DERIK TOLD Sara later, as they were leaving California behind.

"Can't help it," she replied.

"So, what are the chances of that happening?"

"About one in a zillion."

"That's what I thought. Nice truck, though."

"*Great* truck."

"You're looking smug again."

"Sorry."

15

"OKAYYY... WE'VE GOT SLEEPING BAGS, A COOLER, water, backpacks, flashlights, toilet paper, Purell, a first aid kit, dehydrated snacks, a couple of sharp knives, eating utensils, plates, cups, a grill, a frying pan, and a pot. Let's see, what am I forgetting?"

"The fact that I'm a werewolf," Derik muttered, so as not to be overheard.

"Oh, yeah. That. I didn't forget it, I'm just totally discounting it."

"Nice!"

"Quit it, now, you're making me lose track." She squinted at her list, pretending Derik wasn't heaving with indignation less than six inches away. Like Wal-Mart wasn't distracting enough . . . the camping section was bigger than Yosemite.

"Okay, so, we can hit the grocery story for hot dogs, bacon, bread, and—"

"Sara, we don't need all this junk." He fingered the sleeping bag and practically sniffed in disgust. "First off, we have a limited amount of money, so I'll tell you what you don't have to waste the bucks on."

"Oh, would you? That would be swell." She rolled her eyes.

"I can see in the dark, so don't bother with the flashlights. I sure as shit don't need the Band-Aids in the first aid kit. And I'd rather eat my own shit than touch one of those dehydrated beef stews."

"You're so gross," she told him. "And you're forgetting about me. I can neither see in the dark, nor bring my bleating prey down by the neck at a dead run. And I like to be warm at night."

"Why don't you leave that to me?" he leered.

"Why don't you go fuck yourself?"

He deflated. "Aw, c'mon, Sara, it's my job to look out for you. You don't need all this junk."

"Mmmm." She crossed a few more items off the list. "Look, I appreciate that you've aborted the whole 'Kill Sara' plan, I really do. But if I'm going to travel across the country with a homicidal stranger—that's right, I said homicidal, don't puff up like a cobra and glare—then I'm going to take care of myself. Just like I've been doing all along. If you don't mind." *And even if you do, Studboy.*

"That was a good speech," he said admiringly.

"Oh, shut up. And grab that bug spray, will you?"

"Ech! You're not going to actually spray that *on* you, are you?"

"No, I'm going to use it to sweeten my coffee. Just grab it," she said, already exhausted. Long day. Long fucking day, and that was a fact.

"YOU NEED SALT CRYSTALS AND FRESH GROUND pepper? And vanilla sticks?" Derik cried. "I thought we were roughing it!"

"We are, but there are some things I refuse to give up. I think I've been a pretty good sport up 'til now, don't you? I mean, you turned my whole life upside down, but I'm playing along. Look, think of it as bringing a little taste of home along with us on the road."

"I'm thinking of it as a big goddamned waste of money and space, how about that?"

"A person of limited imagination," she admitted, "and poor cooking skills might think of it like that."

He sniffed the jar that held the vanilla pods and tossed it into her cart. "FYI, sunshine, I am a great damned cook, and these things are a total waste on a camping trip. Not to mention, they're from Mexico, not Madagascar, so on top of everything else, you're getting screwed."

"Say that after you've tried my campfire cocoa."

"Sure I will. How much money do we have left, anyway?"

"Enough to get free range eggs," she said, plucking them out of the dairy section. "Be a good boy and scamper off to get some Asiago cheese, will you?"

"I'm going to pretend you didn't say that," he said, folding his arms across his chest.

"You're just mad because we skipped the Milk Bones aisle."

"Sara, for the love of God . . . if you don't stop with the dog jokes, and I mean, stop with them right now . . ." He followed her, practically wringing his hands, and she hid a smile. It was good to have the upper hand, however momentarily.

Camping across country with a werewolf . . . now *that* was going to be an adventure.

PART TWO

Sorceress and Werewolf

16

"SO YOU WANT TO STOP?"

"I don't mind stopping."

"I didn't ask if you'd *mind*. I asked—"

"Since I'm sitting right next to you," he said, trying not to snap, "I was sorta able to follow the conversation. Look, I can go all night. Drive," he added when she went red. "I can drive all night. If you want to, curl up in the back, go to sleep."

"Well, we bought all this camping equipment."

"You. *You* bought it all."

"Right. And it's"—she looked at her wrist—"eight-thirty. We could stop, maybe sleep for a few hours."

"And make some burgers?"

"What?" she cried. "We just dropped twenty bucks at McDonalds!"

"Oh, Big Macs," he scoffed. "They're more like an appetizer than an actual meal."

"Actually," she said frostily, "if memory serves, someone insisted we stop so he could get the toy in the Happy Meal."

"It's for my friend's kid," he tried not to whine. "Anyway, it's not my fault. That stuff doesn't fill you up. Half an hour later—"

"It's been twenty minutes."

"—and you're hungry again."

She smacked herself in the forehead, which looked painful, and left a red mark. He resisted the urge to kiss it. "Okay, okay. So, we'll stop, eat, and sleep. For a little while. We're out of California, anyway. I mean, we're making good time."

"Okay," he said, because really, he didn't know what else *to* say. She was getting nervous, which was making *him* nervous. Which he couldn't stand. It's like she hadn't really thought about the fact that they'd be sleeping right next to each other in the back of a truck until just a couple of minutes ago. Which was extremely weird, because Sara was many things, and stupid wasn't one of them. Shit, it was the first thing that went through *his* mind when they were deciding which nylon bags to buy. "So, we'll stop."

She pointed. "There's a campground."

"Yeah, I see it."

TWENTY MINUTES LATER, THEY HAD THEIR ONE-night camping permit and had selected a teeny campsite that was roughly, given what he'd just paid, ten bucks a square foot.

He decided to kiss her again, break the ice. Well, that, and he wanted to kiss her again. But really, it was, like, a necessity. If she got any edgier, and thus bitchier, he just might try to kill her again, and another brain aneurysm he did *not* need.

So, they'd kiss, and maybe it'd lead to something and maybe not, but she seemed to expect *something*, and he was certainly more than willing to oblige.

Except.

Except, she hopped down from the truck,

groped in one of the bags, and was now coating herself head to foot with noxious chemicals. He coughed and gagged and waved the air in front of his face, to no avail. The cloud was suffocating him!

"Enough, enough!"

"Do you *see* all the mosquitoes?" she cried. "We'll get eaten alive."

"Speak for yourself."

"Are you serious?" She walked over to him, and he backed up, terrified—she was a walking biohazard—but she grabbed his arm, forestalling his retreat. He was coughing so hard he missed her question.

"What?"

"It's true! You don't have a mark on you."

"Bugs don't like werewolves."

"Lucky bastard," she muttered.

"Listen, Sara . . ." She was still holding on to him, which he kind of liked. He bent in. "You know, we're going to be spending a lot of . . . um . . . you know, *time* together . . . and . . . and . . . shit."

"What?" She was looking up into his eyes,

and oh, she was just so pretty it was a damn crime, that's what it was, and . . .

Shit.

His lungs exploded. Or, at least, that's what it felt like.

"You've got to lay off the bug spray," he gasped after about ten minutes of spasms.

"Well, what do you know about that," she said, and smiled for the first time in half an hour. "It's werewolf repellent."

He laughed in spite of himself. "Deep Woods Off: For those really pesky werewolves."

An hour later, he wasn't laughing. They'd eaten, doused their fire, said their good nights, crawled into their sleeping bags. Well, she did. He couldn't see how she could cocoon herself in a heavy bag when it was eighty degrees outside—humans were *weird*, or maybe it was just females of any species—but whatever. And now he was lying beside her in the back of the truck, slowly going insane.

He'd dated humans before, so it wasn't like he'd never had this problem before. The communication thing. Because he had. But somehow, back then, with other women, it hadn't bothered him so much.

It bothered him now.

If Sara were a werewolf, she'd smell his intent and he'd smell hers, and they'd do it, or she'd say right out: Not interested, pal, take a hike, and they wouldn't do it. Period. The end. But Sara couldn't smell a thing, comparably speaking, and what was worse, she was pretending like she didn't know he was so horny he was ready to have sex with his rolled up sleeping bag. So it was this big—this big *thing* that they weren't talking about. What was that saying? It was the elephant in the room. A big, green, horny elephant.

He tried to think: What would Michael do? Jeannie had driven the poor guy nuts in the beginning . . . still did, sometimes. And a lot of the early problems were because she had trouble settling into the Pack. And Michael, as alpha, expected her to fall in line. And Jeannie, as a human who carried firearms, thought he should drop dead. So Michael had a lot of experience with the communication thing. He'd been forced to learn, poor bastard. What would *he* do?

He'd talk to Sara, that's what he'd do.

"Sara," Derik whispered.

Nothing.

"Listen, Sara—" I really really like you, and you smell great, and I think your powers are really cool, if kind of terrifying, and oddly enough this makes you more appealing than any female I've ever known, and I definitely think we should fuck—oh, shit, I mean make love, you know, whatever—and then we can cuddle and I can get SOME FUCKING SLEEP.

"Sara?"

A light snore for an answer.

"Shit."

Saving the world was going to be harder than he thought.

17

"THIS WEREWOLF THING," SARA SAID ABRUPTLY. SHE puffed a hank of hair out of her face and took a break from struggling with her sleeping bag. It was uncanny. You bought the thing in this nice little roll, and after you used it, you couldn't get it back into that nice little roll if someone stuck a gun in your ear. Uncanny! "You know, the full moon's in a couple of days."

"Seventy-eight hours. Yeah, I know."

"So . . . what then?"

"Sara, we could all be dead in seventy-eight hours."

"How many times do I have to tell you?" she snapped. "I'm not going to destroy the world.

And what's with you this morning, you big blond grump?"

He mumbled something. It sounded like "I know you are but what am I?" but even he wouldn't be that immature. And boy, had *he* woken up on the wrong side of the truck this morning!

"I'm just curious about what would happen, is all," she said. "What if you lose control and bite me?"

"What if I do?" he grumped.

"Oh, very nice! Think *I* want to be worried about full moons and biting people and—and getting rabid and eating undercooked food and maybe getting Mad Werewolf Disease?"

He covered his face with his hands and squatted by the smoldering remains of their fire. "It's sooo early . . ."

"Seriously, Derik."

"I am being serious. It's too early for this shit." He took his hands down from his face. "Besides, it's not the flu, Sara. You can't catch it. I could give you a blood transfusion, and you wouldn't catch it. We're two different species."

"Oh. I didn't know that. So all the movies are wrong?"

"Totally, totally wrong." He scrubbed his face with his hands and yawned. "Don't waste your time watching them, unless it's for entertainment value. Also, we don't carry babies off in the moonlight, and I wouldn't eat a person on a bet. Yech."

"Yech?"

He shuddered, and she took offense. "What's wrong with eating a person? You should be so lucky! Not that I want you to."

"You taste terrible, that's what. All of you. The omnivore diet . . . blurgh." He actually gagged!

"Well, nobody's asking you to eat anybody."

"I'd make an exception," he grumbled.

"Very funny. Don't even think about eating me. And if we're two different species, how do you have children with humans? And speaking of blood transfusions, would one of those even take?"

"Yes, and yes. It doesn't happen all the time—cubs with a human—but it does happen. I don't know why, I'm not a goddamned biologist." He groaned again and got up, then loped off toward the truck. "Are we ready? Let's go. Ready?"

"What's the rush? And why are you so scratchy this morning?"

"Couldn't sleep," he replied shortly, stomping on the clutch and starting the truck with a roar. "Went for a walk. All night."

"Well, excuuuse me, Mr. Insomniac—wait!" She ran to throw the last sleeping bag into the back of the truck. "Nobody told me werewolves were such rotten morning people!" She lunged, and just managed to pop the door open as he accelerated.

"Well, now you know," he said, shifting into second as she slammed her door.

"So, what's the plan, Grumpy McGee? Besides a second, possibly third, breakfast by ten o'clock?"

"Drive until we're tired. Stop again. Eat. Sleep. Drive more. Find Arthur's Chosen. Kick their asses. The end."

"A fine plan," she said.

"Except . . ."

"What?"

He yawned again, which was startling—his

jaw stretched wider than she thought would be possible, and he showed a lot of teeth. "Well, I have to stay in touch with my people, or they'll start to worry about me. Maybe send someone else out here. So I thought tonight we'd stay at a safe house." This was a rather small lie. He didn't have to stay in the safe house; he could check in from the road. But the thought of having Sara in a warm bed . . . having Sara . . .

"What? I didn't catch that."

"I said okay," she repeated. "I don't mind sleeping with a roof over my head. Don't yawn anymore."

"Huh? Never mind. And a shower. You should shower so you get all the bug spray—"

"Yes, *fine*, all right. So, we stay at a safe house."

"Well, the thing is, I'd have to explain you. Because if any other werewolf ever found out who you were, they'd try to kill you."

"A possibility to be avoided at all costs," she agreed. "So what do you suggest?"

"Pose as my future mate—my fiancée, I mean."

"Oh."

"I have to tell them something," he explained.

"Well. Okay. I guess. I'm against being killed, you know—I'm not totally irrational. We'll just have to hide the fact that we don't know each other very well."

"Um." He cleared his throat. "There's one other small problem."

"Small, huh?" She sighed as he slowed down and took the exit for Burger King. Like he hadn't just eaten a pound and a half of bacon! "I'll bet. Well, bring it on. The week I'm having, I can take it."

"The thing is, they'll know—my people will know—if we're not really, um, intimate."

Her mind processed this, then decided, the week she'd had, she could *not* take it. Probably she had misunderstood. "What?"

"Well, like I said, they'll know if we aren't, you know, sleeping together. So we have to if we're going to pull this off. Sleep together, I mean."

She turned in her seat to glare at him. He kept his eyes steadily on the road, she noticed. Coward. "You're telling me I have to *fuck* you in order to stay at the safe houses?"

"Yeah."

"Well, too damned bad," she snapped, ignoring the surge of heat to her cheeks.

"You'd rather have your neck broken at the safe house?" he snapped back.

"Yes, upon careful consideration, I think that would be preferable!"

"Oh, stop with the drama queen thing. It's just sex, that's all, just sex, sex, that all it is, and frankly, I'm kind of insulted that you'd rather be gutted than see me naked!"

"They're called standards, pal. And I can't help it if I'm one of the few who didn't tumble into bed within five minutes of first meeting you!"

"Standards!"

"Want me to find a dictionary, blondie?"

"I want you to be a realist," he growled.

"In other words, drop your pants and save your life."

"Anything sounds bad if you say it like *that*."

"Forget it."

He pounded the steering wheel, which groaned alarmingly. "Damn it, Sara, you are the most hardheaded, stubborn, infuriating, annoying, stuck-up, curliest, annoying—"

"Curliest?"

"Aw, shut up. Fine, it's your head. We'll sleep out in the woods again, no touchie. And again. And again. Homo sapiens, man, fucking hothouse flowers, I swear to God."

"I am not," she said automatically, inwardly crushed. She'd sort of been looking forward to a shower. And a bed. She'd gone camping quite a bit as a girl, but now that she was in her late twenties, her idea of roughing it was a Super 8 and a hair dryer.

She cleared her throat and then asked timidly, "Can't—can't you just tell them that because I'm not a—a werewolf, you're still working on getting me into bed?"

He hesitated, then shook his head. "Our kind doesn't make a life-commitment without, uh—"

"Sampling the merchandise?"

"Uh, yeah. I mean, it's a totally natural thing to us. We don't have this whole Victorian attitude toward sex that you guys do. And the thing is, I wouldn't bring a casual date to a safe house."

"Oh."

He shrugged. "So, okay. We'll keep camping. I guess I shouldn't have sprung it on you like that, but I thought it'd be worse if I didn't say anything until we were at the house."

She actually shivered at the thought. "No, that's a good point. Well . . . what's a safe house like?"

"It's a house where a werewolf family lives and they take in guests a lot. People on the run, or on a mission, or even making a go-see trip to the Cape to meet Michael and Lara."

"Lara being . . ."

"The next Pack leader."

"Oh. You don't run a patriarchic society?"

"I don't think so," he said doubtfully.

"Who's Lara again?"

"Michael's daughter."

"Ah! Dynastic, then. Never mind. So it wouldn't be . . . weird . . . if we just showed up at this place and asked to spend the night."

"No. It'd be normal."

"But we'd have to share a bed."

"Yup."

"Actually, we'd have to do it before we showed up at the safe house, right? So the other werewolves could tell we'd been intimate? Not that it's any of their damn business," she added in a mutter.

There was a long pause, and then Derik answered, sounding almost like he was strangling. "Yes, we'd have to do it before we showed up."

She drummed her fingers on the seat and watched the scenery go by. "Well. I'm really not that kind of girl."

"Oh, I know," he said earnestly.

"But you're kind of cute."

"Really?" He seemed pleased.

"In an overbearing, totally obnoxious sort of way," she explained, watching him deflate a bit. "And we *are* on a mission to save the world."

He didn't say anything, just pulled into the BK parking lot.

"We could talk about it, I guess. I mean . . . I'd like a shower."

"And I'd like for you to have a shower."

"Bastard," she muttered.

18

THEY WERE STILL DEBATING THE MERITS OF LOVE-making—or not—when he pulled up to the Kwik N' Go. "Gotta use the phone," he explained.

"How?"

"Huh?"

"The phone," Sara said. She still reeked strongly of bug spray, but driving around for hours with the windows open had alleviated some of the damage. At least he could think about kissing her without gagging—a crucial step. And the wind had tossed her curls around and around; she looked like an adorable red dandelion. "You can't use your cell phone, for obvious reasons. But how are you paying for a phone call to the Cape from *here*? You can't use your credit card."

"Oh."

"And you can't call from the safe house?"

"They'd hear me anywhere in the house," he admitted.

"Oh. Creepy. I suppose calling collect is out of the question?"

"Only if you don't mind a bunch of were-wolves tracking you down."

"Okay, well, let's try this." She hopped out of the truck and walked up to the pay phone on the sidewalk. "This works for me sometimes," she explained over her shoulder. "I used pay phones a lot before I got my cell, and it usually worked out."

She picked up the receiver, listened, then asked, "What's the number?"

He told her.

She tapped in the number, listened, then handed him the phone. "It's ringing."

He took the receiver from her, staring. It *was* ringing. "Won't it ask me for change, or—"

"Wyndham residence."

"Oh, hi, Moira. Listen—"

"Derik! Hey, where the hell are you? How's it going? Are you okay? Michael's been going out of his mind, here! Me, too," she added.

"Tracking her down has been a little harder than I thought," he said with a nervous glance at Sara. Thank God, thank God Moira wasn't anywhere near him. She'd smell a lie, and then kick his ass righteous. He'd deserve it, too. He couldn't remember ever lying before. It was a waste of time in the Pack. It made him feel like a real rat turd now. "But I'm closing in. Just wanted to let everyone know I'm okay. Got that? I'm okay, everything's fine right now. Tell Mike, okay?"

"Okay, honey. Things out here are fine, too. We're basically hanging around, waiting to get the word, you know? So you take care of yourself, okay?"

"Sure. Um, patch me through to Antonia?"

"Sure. She's had a migraine since you left," Moira warned, which made Derik cringe—Antonia was a bear when she was feeling fine—"so I'm not sure she'll be good company, to put it very, *very* mildly, but here she comes, so hold on to your fur." There was a click as he was put on hold.

"I guess this phone's screwed up," he said to Sara. "It's not asking for change or anything."

"Guess so," she replied, looking smug.

"You're scary," he said, and then, "Hello?"

"What are you *doing*? Owww!" Antonia complained. "My head, goddamn it!"

"Well, don't yell if you've got a migraine," he said reasonably. "Listen, Antonia—"

"You chimp, what the *hell* are you doing?"

"Saving the world," he replied shortly. "My own way. And don't call me that."

"But *she's right there!*"

"Duh. Listen, don't tell Mike, okay?"

"Aw, man, Derik, you're killing me," she complained. "You are *fucking* killing me!"

For a moment he actually thanked God that Antonia had a persecution complex. She was one of the few Pack members who would actually consider helping him deceive Michael. Moira, for example, would never, ever do it. She'd feel bad, she'd apologize the whole time she was kicking his ass and then dragging him by the scruff of the neck to take his medicine, but friendship was one thing, and Pack was Pack.

"Look, Antonia, I wouldn't let you twist in the wind on this. We've got a plan. I'm pretty sure it will work."

"*Pretty sure?* Owww!"

"Look, I must be on the right track, or you would have ratted me out to Mike by now, right? I mean, your visions must be showing you that something's going right. Right?"

Sullen silence.

"Right," he repeated, on slightly surer ground. "So, listen, I'm okay, she's okay, and we're gonna get the bad guys and save the world. See, I think the bad guys will accidentally trick her into destroying the world, so if we take care of them, we take care of anybody else."

"And how the blue hell do you know that?"

"Well, I don't. Know it, exactly. You know, like you know two plus two makes four. But I feel it. I mean, I know Sara would never do something that bad on purpose. So the bad guys must do it, or trick her into doing it, or something."

"You're talking out your ass. And besides, you're not an alpha, Derik," Antonia pointed out through gritted teeth. "It's not your call. I mean . . . you could run a Pack, but Michael's the boss of this Pack, and he told you what to do. And *you're not doing it*."

"Just . . . don't say anything yet, okay?"

"Derik . . ." This was more a howl than a groan.

"Antonia."

"You're fucking crazy, you *know* you're crazy, right?"

"Just do this one thing for me."

"Sure," she snapped. "The first favor he ever asks me in twenty-two years, and *this* is it!"

For a moment he was startled . . . Antonia was so annoying, so bitchy, so harassed because of her visions, it was easy to forget she was still just a baby. She was barely voting age, and look what he was asking of her!

"Thanks," he said, because that was her way of saying yes. "I owe you one."

"You owe me *twenty*, you big, stupid, lumbering, asshole moronic—" He hung up on her. The conversation had gone as well as he could have hoped; no need to drag it out.

"Okay," he said, letting out a deep breath. "I bought us some time, anyway."

Sara smiled at him. It was the first smile of the day—they'd spent the afternoon screeching at each other in between bouts of fast food—and it knocked him out all over again, how gorgeous she was, how funny, how cute, how—"Yeah, sounds like you did. Thanks. What do you say we go find this safe house of yours?"

"Great," he said. "Showers all around."

"Enough rubbing in how bad I smell," she muttered, trailing him to the truck.

"I just meant that I could use a shower, too."

"Sure you did."

19

THEY HAD EATEN (TWICE, IN DERIK'S CASE), DRUNK cocoa, and roasted marshmallow after marshmallow. Sara knew if she gobbled one more soft white squishy candy she would explode. But she couldn't stop herself from eating them.

Quit stalling, she ordered herself.

Ugh, she answered herself.

"Okay," she said thickly, noticing Derik was watching her with amazement. "Let's do it before I lose my nerve."

"How romantic," he commented. He was crouched over the fire, balanced on the balls of his feet. "Are you all right? You look a little . . . bloated."

"Do me," she commanded, and stripped off her shirt. Her belly, bulging with marshmallows, pooched out over the waistband of her jeans. "You know you want to."

"Uh . . . right this minute? I wouldn't bet the farm. Maybe you should lie down."

"No, no, no. We're gonna do it. We *have* to do it, to save the world." She groaned and massaged her belly. "And to sleep in a warm bed tomorrow night. And to have a shower! Think of it, all that warm water . . . and soap, think of the soap!"

"I can't do this," he announced. "It's too much like taking advantage."

"You're right about that, but I'll be the one— hurp!—taking advantage. Now get over here." She painfully wiggled out of her jeans, then lay, gasping like a landed trout, beside the fire.

Derik was trying not to laugh, and as a result his face had gone an alarming shade of apple-red. "I don't think you're up to this tonight," he gasped.

"Aw, shaddup, when I want you to think, I'll yank your leash."

"Now you're just being mean."

"Whatever works, pal. Now strip."

"Oh, it's like that? Strip?"

She reached out and cupped the warm bulge in his jeans. "Like you're not dying to."

"Well, that's true," he said, and quit arguing, and in a minute he was naked, and helping her out of her bra and panties—

"What's burning?"

"Your bra . . . sorry."

—and then they were rolling in the grass beside the truck, kissing and groping and moaning and for a minute Sara forgot about her grotesquely distended belly, and the mosquitoes munching on her legs.

And then he was easing inside her and that was fine—it was a little uncomfortable, because he was large and she wasn't ready, but it was all right, because she just wanted this over with, but oh, oh, she hadn't expected it to feel good, she hadn't expected . . . expected this.

He rocked against her, obligingly smacking the mosquitoes he saw on her, and then his rocking speeded up, and she wriggled in the grass to give him better access, and then he stiffened all over, the cords on his neck standing out like steel.

"Ooofta," she said when he collapsed over her.

"I swear," he mumbled into her neck. "I swear I'm usually much better at this."

"No, no, it's all right. Speed impresses me!"

"Sara, you're killing me."

She laughed, and stroked the back of his neck.

20

"HI, I'M—JON?"

Sara poked him in the side. "Your name's Derik," she whispered.

He ignored her—and embraced the red-haired man in the doorway so hard, the poor guy left his feet. "Jon, you son of a bitch! I thought that was your scent!"

"Never mind my mother," the other man replied, laughing. "Or my scent. And put me down. Derik, what the hell are you doing here?"

"It's a long story," he said, jerking a thumb over his shoulder at Sara. "This is my fiancée. We need a place to crash for the night. Okay?"

His old friend's face lit up like a moonrise. "Shit, yes, okay! Can you stay longer?"

Derik shook his head and trailed the shorter man into the house. Sara, after a doubtful look around, followed. "Got to get to the coast. Long story, which I won't bore you with. What are you doing in Kansas?"

"Hi," Jon said, extending a hand for Sara to shake. "I'm Jon; Derik and I grew up together, and he's still got no manners at all. Welcome to my home."

"Thank you," she said, jerking her head to get her hair out of her eyes. She thought about trying to straighten the mess and immediately dismissed it as a lost cause.

Jon was a redhead, too, except his hair was a rich, deep auburn, cut brutally short, and his eyes were the green of old Coke bottles. He was a couple of inches shorter than Derik; in fact, exactly her height. It was disconcerting to say the least, being able to look him straight in the eyes. His pupils, she noted clinically, were enormous. She had to swallow against the sudden blockage in her throat. Were all werewolves so . . . unsettling and charismatic? And green-eyed? "I'm Sara," she managed at last. "It's nice to be here. Nice to meet you, I mean." She noticed Jon trying not to wrinkle his nose, and sighed. "I'll let you two catch up. Meantime, can I use your shower?"

"SO, WHAT THE HELL?" DERIK HAD POLISHED OFF the last of his steak tartare, and was now rooting through Jon's fridge for a beer. "Last I heard, you got mated, Shannon was pregnant, and you were off to see the world. Now you're here? And where's the rest of the family?"

"Visiting Shannon's mother." Jon shuddered. "I decided to pass. I don't like talking to grumpy old women who are hairy when the moon *isn't* full. I'm sorry you couldn't see my cub, though."

"Heard you had a girl? Katie?"

"Mm-hmm. She's got my eyes and Shannon's brains, so that worked out nicely."

"Very nicely," he agreed, still rooting. "Listen, how come you left in the first place?" *Ah! Hello, beer, my old friend, I've come to glug you once again.* He twisted the bottle cap off—werewolves disdained bottle openers—and took a deep drink.

"Oh, yeah, that's the stuff. Oooh, baby. Anyway, how come you left? We all wondered."

"Well, you know how it is." Jon had been tipped back in his kitchen chair, now he brought it forward until all four legs were on the floor. "I mean, you're not there now," he pointed out. "You can love the Pack but not necessarily want to be with them every second. I needed a little space. The mansion, big as it was, felt crowded after I mated."

"I can relate. Mike and me almost got into a huge fight before I left."

"Over what?"

"Over nothing."

"Come on, cough up."

"It was stupid."

"Did it have anything to do with you being an alpha now?" Jon asked quietly.

"What, did Moira put it in the newsletter?"

"No. You're different. You walk different, stand different . . . even smell a little different. I bet Michael knew before you did and just waited for you to figure it out."

"Well, we almost tore each other's heads off. I

had to get the hell out of there before I did something really stupid. Even for me."

Jon pondered that one in silence, while Derik finished the beer. Finally, he said, "It's a dangerous business, I guess. Sometimes. You're lucky you didn't really fight. The last thing you need is to be running the Pack. Also," he added matter-of-factly, "Jeannie would have shot you in the face."

Derik shrugged.

"And now you're with that cute, curly haired redhead."

"Yeah."

"Human, huh? Well, congratulations."

"Thanks."

"You don't seem like a happy mate-to-be, you'll excuse me for pointing it out."

"We've been fighting a lot." Finally, an unvarnished truth! "She might be having second thoughts."

Jon shook his head. "She hasn't even had first thoughts. How long have you guys known each other?"

"Never mind."

"So, less than a week."

"Never *mind*, you nosy S.O.B."

"Swept her off her feet, huh?"

"Something like that," Derik said lamely.

"Uh-huh."

"Well, it was." He'd thought it would be bad, trying to fool a regular Pack member, but this was Jon. Practically his littermate! Of all the safe houses in all the world, why'd he have to walk into Jon's? "It's been kind of a stressful week."

"Mmm. You know what your mom always said."

"If you chew on my hardwood floors one more time, I'll break your neck?"

"The other thing."

"Yeah," he said sourly. "Stick to your own kind."

Jon spread his hands, but didn't say anything.

21

"SO!" SARA SAID BRIGHTLY, BOUNCING INTO THE living room, which was floor-to-ceiling windows on the entire west side. She'd thought Kansas was supposed to be flat and boring, but it had a kind of wild beauty about it—like a prairie rose. And the windows in this place! Werewolves must not like being unable to see out. Well, of course she already knew that from Mr. "Can't we please get a convertible?" "What should we do?"

Derik, the big dope, nearly fell out of his chair. "What? Now? What are you talking about?"

"It's only nine o'clock, calm down," she said. "Do you guys want to watch a movie? Play a game?"

"A game?" Jon asked. He was a yummy one, all right, with that build and that hair and those green, green eyes. No Derik, of course, but who was? He was a watcher, though, while Derik was a doer. She could tell . . . Jon didn't say much, but his eyes were always calculating, judging, weighing. She pitied the house burglar who tried to crack *this* place. "What kind of game?"

"I don't know . . . this is *your* house. Whatcha got?"

"The only games we have are Candyland and Chutes and Ladders," Jon admitted.

"Oh, you have a little girl, that's right—I saw the pictures in the hall. She's adorable." Adorable, with about six hundred too many teeth. A truly frightening smile for a four-year-old. "Really darling."

"Thank you. Shouldn't you guys—um—aren't you tired? Don't you want to go to bed?"

"No," Sara said, at the exact moment Derik said, "Yes."

"Uh-huh," Jon said, narrowing his eyes at Sara. "Tell me again why you guys are—"

"Deck of cards?" she said hurriedly. "You've got to have one of those lying around."

"Right!" Derik said heartily. "I could really go for a—a game of—um—"

"Cards!" Sara said brightly.

Jon sighed and got up. "I think I can find one around here somewhere. Be right back."

Once he left, Derik muttered, "Very smooth."

"Shh! I thought you said he could hear everything."

"He can. When are we going to bed?"

"When you stop being an asshole." She glanced at her watch. "Shouldn't take more than a few years."

"Very f—"

"Here we are," Jon said with fake heartiness.

"This isn't such a great idea," Derik said.

"Horny bastard," Sara muttered.

"Well, yeah, but besides that."

"Don't be such a spoilsport." Jon sat down on the end of the couch and pulled the coffee table closer to them. Though the tension was thick enough to swim through, he ignored it and, ever the polite host, handed the cards to Sara. "One or two games, big deal."

Sara was blinking in confusion. "What are you guys talking about?"

"Sare-Bear, we've sort of—"

"Got to stop calling me that."

"—got the advantage. I mean, you can't bluff us. We'll know it. Your body language gives it away, even your smell changes."

"Gross," she commented.

"We'll always know when you have a good hand or a bad hand. It's not really fair. Now checkers . . . we could play checkers . . ."

"That's okay," she said. "Cards will pass the time. Consider me warned."

"Seriously," Jon said, shifting uncomfortably on his end of the couch. "It's like playing cards when we can see your cards, but you can't see ours. Not very sporting."

. "Oh, hush up and deal. It'll be fun. What are we playing for? Got any quarters?"

"OH, BOY," DERIK SAID HALF AN HOUR LATER.

Sara, stacking her quarters, didn't look up.

"Let me get this straight, no pun intended," Jon said. "In ten hands, you've been dealt a full house, queens over jacks, a straight, a straight flush, four aces, another straight flush, another full house, aces over kings, and another four of a kind. Aces again."

"What can I say? Lady luck likes me."

"Uh-huh."

"Told you it'd be fun."

"Uh-huh. Derik, can I talk to you a minute?"

"No," Derik said.

"Now."

"That's what I said, now. You just misheard. Back in a minute, Sara."

"You, uh, want me to come with?" she said, nervously watching Jon grab Derik by the shoulder and haul him away.

"No! Don't go near him. I mean, I'll be fine. I mean—"

Then they were in the hall, and then they were in the office with the door closed.

"Okay," Jon said.

"Now, Jon—"

"What the hell are you up to?"

"Shh! Sara will hear."

"She couldn't hear if I left the door open, and you know it. What's going on?"

"You wouldn't believe me if I told you."

Jon glared, and Derik didn't drop his gaze. Finally, Jon dropped his and said to the floor, "For the record, you're both full of shit. You're not engaged, you barely know each other. You're hiding something huge, and there's something weird about your lady friend. *Really* weird. I can't put my finger on it . . . can't even get my nose around it . . . but it's making me really nervous." He rubbed the back of his neck, frowning.

"Like I said. You wouldn't believe it." Derik could feel his heart rate—which had been trip-hammering at about one-eighty—slow down once Jon quit challenging him. Maybe this wouldn't be ugly. Maybe—

Jon dragged his gaze up. "Derik, you're my friend, we grew up together. So I'm giving you the benefit of the doubt, here. And I don't want to fight, and I don't want to call Michael."

"Well, shit, Jon, I don't want to fight either."

"Uh-huh. But you better get your thumb out and do whatever the fuck it is you're supposed to do. I have a family."

Derik nodded. "I know, Jon. Mike has one, too, and it's like my own family. *You're* like my own family. You think I'd screw around if it meant hurting you, or someone important to you? I'd never do that. I'd kill myself before I'd do that."

"Finally," Jon commented, "a truth."

"Look, I'm not sure what's going to happen myself yet, but I've got it covered." *I think.*

"Maybe I can help. Can you tell me about it?"

"Not really. It's hard to explain, but Sara and me—we make a good team. She can—you wouldn't believe it. But we're gonna do the right thing. She'll see to it, and I'll see to it. I swear it on my life, man. Not your family's, or Mike's, or Lara's life . . . *my own life.*"

There was a long, tense moment, and then Jon relaxed. "All right, Der. We've known each other too long not to trust each other when it gets down to the wire. Do you need help? I can come with you if—"

"No!" Christ, no. He didn't want Jon anywhere *near* Arthur's Chosen when it went down. Bad enough he and Sara were going to be there. "No, you stay here. Take care of your family. I'll come back and tell you all about it, when we're done."

"Swear."

"Swear."

Jon nibbled his lower lip, cut his eyes away for a moment, then finally said, "All right, then."

DERIK STAGGERED DOWN THE HALLWAY. HE'D GOTten away with it! Jon knew—it had been stupid to even try to fool him—but the sensible bastard was letting it ride. It wasn't the first time Derik had thanked God for Jon's basic levelheadedness. Werewolves really did have it better . . . Jon knew Derik was good for his word, and thus the unpleasantness of a fight to the death was avoided. Good deal!

Even better, he and Sara didn't have to have sex, which sucked for him but was nice for her, so that was—

He tapped on the door and walked into the guest room, just in time to see Sara drop her robe and slip between the covers. He got a tantalizing flash of cream-colored skin and streaming red curls, and then she was snuggled beneath the quilt.

"There you are," she whispered. "Close the door."

He did.

"Come over here."

He did.

"Well, come on."

"Uh?"

"Let's get this over with." Then she blushed to her hairline. "Sorry, I didn't mean it to sound like that. But let's do this before your friend gets any more suspicious. I was really worried about you when he whisked you away."

He was trying not to rock back on the heels; he couldn't get the smell of roses out of his nose. Not that he wanted to. Except he better. Yeah. Because if he didn't—"Uh . . . we . . . uh . . ."

She threw the quilt back, and he could see her bare leg, bent at the knee, the pale joint inviting kisses, inviting—

"Come *on*," she said impatiently. "Before I lose my nerve, or your friend gets any nutty ideas."

"Okay," he said, and was out of his clothes in about six seconds. He ignored the twinges— okay, the big giant pokes—of conscience. It wasn't as hard as he thought it would be.

Her knee . . . that's what did it. It was as erotic to him as if she'd dropped the sheet and shown

him her tits. And her smell. Her wonderful sweet
smell. She was like—like dessert.

You'll pay for this one later, his inner voice,
the one that sounded annoyingly like Michael,
informed him. *Oh, boy, will you pay.*

He didn't doubt it. And he couldn't help it. He
was about to dance with possibly the most dangerous woman in the world . . .

. . . and he couldn't wait.

22

I'M ABOUT TO DO IT WITH A WEREWOLF. A WEREWOLF. *Again!* Sara kept saying it in her head, and it kept not working. This was weirder than the time she did it with the UPS guy. That had been like a bad porn movie come to life: "Got a package for you, ma'am." "Oooooh, a package! Bring it over here, stud." And then, natch, she never heard from him again. It was like he'd changed routes or something. Probably he had. But anyway, this had that beat by a country mile. A werewolf. A *werewolf!*

Telling herself this was all part of saving the world didn't work, either. Truth was, Derik was magically delicious, and she meant to have another piece of him. The fact that they *had* to do it was icing on the cake. A big, blond, yummy cake. A big, muscle-y, preternaturally strong, sexy, fabulous cake. A—

Whoa.

He'd stripped in about half a second, and she barely had a glimpse of his ridiculously perfect body—washboard abs, long, long legs, flat stomach, bulging biceps, and a fairly fabulous dick, which jutted up like some sort of orgasm-seeking divining rod—before he was on her.

"Oh my God," he said, and then his mouth was on hers, he was tearing the quilt away, his tongue was in her mouth, and then he was nibbling her throat and breathing deeply, as if he couldn't get enough of the way she smelled. "Oh, Jesus."

"Are you going to talk through this whole thing? Because I'm trying to think of England, here."

"Sara, for the love of God, *please* shut up."

"Make me."

Then he was trailing kisses down her throat, her collarbone, her breasts. He played with her nipples until they were stiff and hard, and now she was doing a few "oh my Gods" herself. She squirmed beneath him, trying to give him better access, and gripped his shoulders, which were rigid with strain.

Now he was kissing her stomach, and now her mons, kissing and taking big gulps of air, and, weirdly, he was shuddering like he had a fever. Then he was coming up to her again, grabbing her thighs and slinging her legs over his shoulders. "Sorry," he panted, and then she could feel his cock between her legs, urgent and heartless, and then he was shoving himself inside her.

She shrieked in surprise, then yelled again when he nipped the side of her neck. "Sorry," he groaned again.

And here was the weird part. The weird, sick part. It hurt, sure. It was tight as hell. It had been a while for her—last night barely counted, that was for damn sure. And she was certainly accustomed to more than forty seconds of foreplay.

But she loved it, too. She loved that he was taking her, that he was so overcome by her they weren't playing nice. He needed to fuck her, and so he was.

And she needed to be fucked, and so she was.

He buried his face in her hair and gripped her thighs harder. The bed rocked and squeaked. She felt the change in him as his orgasm approached; his muscles, already rigid with strain, seemed to get even harder for a second, and then he was shaking over her, and then he was done, and couldn't look at her.

"Well," she said, after waiting twenty seconds.

"I swear," he said, still not looking at her. "I swear I don't usually suck so much in bed. I'm aware you've heard that before."

She laughed; she couldn't help it. "It's all right. You seemed, um, like you needed to do it."

"Oh, I needed to do it. And in about ten minutes, I'm gonna need to do it again."

"Gee," she said dryly, ignoring the bolt of excitement that it brought to her belly, "I can hardly wait."

"Nice try," he said, slipping out of her and kissing her deeply, deeply. He sucked on her tongue for a long minute, then added, "But I can tell you like the idea."

"Insufferable bastard," she muttered into his mouth.

"God, you smell *so* good. Anybody ever tell

you? I mean, seriously good." He stretched, and the bed creaked. "They should bottle you."

"I can safely say no one has ever suggested bottling me. So, uh, do you think Jon heard?"

He hesitated. "Well, yeah."

"Okay. I mean, creepy, and I'll be freaking out about this tomorrow, but at least you won't get in trouble."

Another odd hesitation. "Right."

"Breakfast should be fun," she muttered. "But at least that's done, right? So, good."

He didn't answer, just rolled over and kissed her again, then licked her nipples for what seemed like a delightful eternity. He cupped her left breast and brushed his thumb over her nipple again and again, while licking and kissing the other one, and then he would switch, until she was groaning and writhing beneath him.

He went lower, nuzzling between her legs, then separating her folds with his tongue, darting and licking, and then his tongue was inside her and she nearly hit the ceiling.

He settled between her thighs and over her clit and licked steadily for what seemed like an hour, until she was clawing at the bed sheets and whimpering like a maddened animal. Her orgasm hit her like a freight train, and he backed off, then was immediately on her again, spreading her apart with his hands and stroking her with his tongue and even, very very gently, biting her.

When he came up to her again she was more than ready; she wrapped her legs against his waist and was thrusting up at him before he was even seated all the way within her.

"Oh, Christ," he managed, and propped himself up on his hands, and they went at each other for another eternity. She could come again if she tightened her thighs around him as he thrust, and did, and he groaned like he could feel it, feel her coming around him, and after a while she was begging him, begging him to come, and he was nibbling the sweet spot behind her ear and ignoring her, and they were so slick with sweat they were sliding against each other, and finally she bit him on the ear, hard, and that was it, that was what he needed, and then they were done, and it took her about ten minutes to get her breath back.

When she did, she said, "This doesn't mean we're married or anything, right?"

"Unfortunately, no."

"What?"

"I said, no."

"Oh. Okay. That was—" *The best in my life. Probably the best in anybody's life. Good work, old chap!* "That was really great."

"I knew it'd be really great," he said softly, and picked up her hand, and kissed her palm.

"Mmm. Conceited much?"

"Sara. Can I ask you something?"

"Mmm."

"What happened to your mom?"

She squinted at him, trying to see his face in the dark. "Why would you ask me that?"

"I don't know . . : something Dr. Cummings said. Actually, the way you reacted to something he said. It got me wondering."

"Well, she was killed in a stupid accident. And it was her own fault—she wasn't watching where she was going. Plus she was jaywalking."

"Oh. I'm sorry."

"It's against the law for a reason, you know."

"Yeah, okay. Well, I'm sorry," he said again.

"Thanks. What about your folks?"

"They died helping Michael's dad take over the Pack."

"Oh. Well, um, my mom got run over by a garbage truck." Pause. "It's not funny, Derik."

"I'm not laughing."

"You big liar."

"I'm really sorry," he said, sounding truly sincere. "It was just . . . unexpected."

"The really weird thing was, the city paid. I mean, I didn't sue or anything, they just gave me a big check. Just in time," she added glumly, "for me to pay for the first couple years of college."

"Oh."

"Yeah, it was like living in 'The Monkey's Paw.' Gee, I wish I could afford to go to college . . . whoops, my mom's dead, and the city's paying for school."

There was a long pause. "That's creepy."

"Tell me about it," she said, and sighed.

LATER, SARA DOZED OFF, HER SMALL HAND NESTLED on his chest. Derik was wide awake, ignoring the clamoring of his conscience.

Oh my God, that was so so good.

Oh my God, I'm such an asshole.

But it was so good!

And you'll pay for it, ass face. What the hell are you going to tell her? And when? Jerk.

So so good. Like, once in a lifetime good. And her poor mom! I'm glad she told me. Imagine living with—

Stay focused. Jerk.

And oh Jesus, her smell, and the feel of her, the way she held on and whimpered and squirmed, the way—

The way you were a jerk. The way you didn't tell her she didn't have to. The way you didn't want another sleepless night.

Well, look at it this way, he thought. Maybe she'll destroy the world, and I'll never have to tell her tonight was completely unnecessary.

Nice, his inner voice—Michael's voice—said snidely. *Maybe billions will die so you don't have to face the music. You're sick, dude.*

23

DERIK ROLLED OVER AND SAW SARA SITTING ON THE edge of the bed. "Didja blow up the world yet?" he mumbled, scrubbing his face with his palm.

"Stop asking me that. And the answer is no." She took a sip of her coffee and grinned at him. "So you have to get up."

"Aw, man . . ."

"It's ten o'clock in the morning! I'm pretty sure the good guys don't laze away in bed, giving the bad guys plenty of time to plan."

"Ummm . . . can I have a sip of your coffee?"

"Touch my cup and die. Jon's got a whole pot out in the kitchen. Besides, I put a ton of sugar in mine, and you don't like that."

He yawned. "How'd you know that?"

"I pay attention, numb nuts. Rise and shine."

"Ummm . . . c'mere."

She scooted out of his reach. "None of that, now. It's time to go." She smiled at him again. He supposed that in the movies the sun would be shining on her and she'd seem all godlike and bright to him, but this was real life, and so she only looked really really good. She was wearing a scoop-necked T-shirt that tantalized him with her cleavage, and when she smiled, her eyes lit up and looked like the deep end of a pool on a hot day. "Play your cards right, though, and maybe we'll stop early for the day."

"It's a date," he said, and bounded out of bed.

She nearly spilled her coffee. "Jesus! A little warning before you do that."

"Wait until I've had my coffee. Then you'll see something." He yawned again and scratched his ass, then remembered someone he wanted to impress was in the room, and stopped. "Sleep good?"

"After you wore me out last night? I'm sort of surprised I didn't slip into a coma around two A.M."

"Awww," he said, and twined one of her red

curls around his finger. "That's so sweet." He let go, and it bounced into her eye.

"Ow!"

"Oh, shit! Sorry."

"As a tender moment," she informed him, "that left a lot to be desired. Go take a shower."

"Come with me," he wheedled.

"Forget it," she said. "Better hurry, or all the coffee will be gone."

THEY WERE FINISHING BREAKFAST WHEN JON snapped his fingers, said, "Forgot," got up, left, came back. "Picked this up for you when I went out," he said, and slid a glossy magazine across the table.

"Oh, dude! Thanks! I've been waiting for this one." To her complete and total amazement, Derik started thumbing through the current issue of *Fine Cooking*. "I don't even know why I subscribe to this thing, it's really hard to wait for it to show up in the mail. I always end up buying it on the stands, too. Oh, well, I can always sell the extra ones on eBay."

"What just happened?" she asked.

"If you're going to be with Derik," Jon said, "you must also be obsessed with cooking."

"What? Seriously?" She looked at the big, strapping blond across from her. "Big homemaking fan, are you?"

"No," Jon said as Derik became absorbed in an article on cilantro, "but he's a big cooking fan."

"I only get it for the articles," Derik said defensively.

"Didn't you notice the shirt?" Jon added, referring to Derik's black shirt with white lettering: FREE MARTHA.

"I could hardly miss it," she said, "but I thought it was some werewolf thing."

Jon snorted. "To our everlasting relief, it's not."

"Okay, *this* is the weirdest thing to happen to me this week," Sara said.

Derik slapped the magazine closed. "I can't concentrate with you two jabbering like apes."

"Hey, hey!" Jon protested. "Watch the language."

"Sorry. Sara, are you ready to hit it?"

She blinked. "Sure, I guess. Are *you*?"

"I'll cook for you sometime. Then you won't give me shit."

"You've been letting me slave over a hot campfire all this time?"

"I need my kitchen tools to do a really good job," he explained.

"Great. Hey, I love to cook, too. At last, something in common! Not that, as an engaged couple, we don't have tons in common," she added hastily, realizing her slip. "Because we totally, totally do. Have tons in common, I mean. *Tons.*"

"That's quite a hole you're digging with your mouth," Derik observed.

"It's true," Jon supplied, rescuing her. "Derik's an amazing cook. His tomato-less pizza will make you cry like a tiny girl. Don't get me started on his butterscotch cookies."

Sara said nothing. For the life of her, she couldn't think of a thing. Not that she was some sort of reverse chauvinist, all "men shouldn't be in the kitchen because they're too big and strong," but it was hard to picture Derik in a KISS THE COOK apron.

The three of them stood around the table, Derik cradling his magazine, and there was a long, awkward moment, followed by Jon clearing his throat.

"Well, good luck, you guys."

"Thanks for letting us stay over," Sara said, giving him a hug. "And for the, um, reading material."

"Sure, Sara, anytime." Jon was looking at Derik. "Sure you don't want an extra pair of hands?"

"We've got it covered," Derik replied. "And by 'got it covered' I of course mean, we're pulling it out of our asses as we go along."

"But don't worry," Sara added.

"Right. Don't do that."

"At least stay through the full moon," Jon coaxed. "Rest up, figure out the rest of your plan."

"We gotta hit it, Jon. It'll be fine. We'll be in a state park somewhere when She comes up."

"Don't forget your promise," Jon said.

"We'll be back," Derik said.

"We're like terminators that way," Sara added brightly.

24

THEY WERE IN ANOTHER CAMPSITE, SUPPER WAS done, even the dishes were done. Now they were snuggling beside the campfire, and when Sara looked up into his face, she noticed his eyes glowed back yellow-green. It was startling, yet comforting.

"You know, the thing about Jon," she began.

"Oh, good, I was hoping you were going to talk about another guy."

She ignored that. "He seemed like a regular person, you know? I mean, to look at him, you wouldn't think, 'Thar's a werewolf, git the gun, Paw.' "

"Christ, I hope not. And I guess it makes

sense. There's not very many of us. And there's tons of you. So I guess we blend in pretty good."

"I mean, I see you all the time, and I forget about it a lot, unless you do something to remind me. Like this morning. I blinked, and you were on the other side of the room. It freaked me out."

"I can't help it"—he sighed—"if I've evolved as a genetically superior being."

"Oh, shut the hell up. Listen, what's the real reason you're avoiding your family? The Pack?"

"Huh?"

"Well, you just seem awfully concerned that they'll catch up with us, but not just because they'll try to ice me. So what's up with that?"

"It's . . . kind of complicated."

"Derik . . ."

"Well . . . you know what an alpha is, right? Like the boss of a group? And our Pack has an alpha. It's Michael. Which is totally fine. But sometimes . . . sometimes alphas aren't born, they're made. And I don't know how it happened, but in the last couple of weeks I've wanted . . . wanted things I don't deserve. At least I think I don't deserve them. And I left before things could get . . . well, you know."

"Oh."

"I can't go home again. So," he added, forcing cheer, "it's just as well that this whole save-the-world thing came up, you know?"

"Well, what I don't get is—"

"Can we change the subject?"

"Uh . . . sure. So, what's the plan for tomorrow night?"

"Before or after we have hot, wild monkey sex?"

"Can we have a serious talk, here? Like for thirty seconds? Is that too much for you?"

"I can't help it if I'd rather picture you naked than talk about our feelings, or whatever."

"I'm not even talking about our feelings, you half-wit!" She saw that he was delighted he'd teased her into yelling. "Very funny. Are you gonna answer the question?"

"Well. We'll have to make sure we're pulled over by the time the sun goes down, that's all. I'll Change, you'll sleep, I'll probably bring down a couple of rabbits and then curl up next to the fire, blah-blah."

"Blah *blah*? This is the most surreal conversation I've ever had," she announced, "and it's been quite a week for me, in case you hadn't noticed. You'll curl up next to the fire? Like a good boy? Should we pull over and get you some Milk Bones?"

"You know," he grumped, "*some* people would be a little nervous about spending the night in the woods with a werewolf."

"Some people cheat on their taxes. It's a weird world." She slipped her hand under his shirt. His pro-Martha Stewart shirt. Best not to go that route, if she wanted to maintain her horniness. "So, uh, you got any plans for the rest of the evening?"

"Well, I was thinking about jumping your bones and then taking a nap."

"Excellent! Oh, wait a minute, I'm not that easy." Heck, two nights ago she'd been fervently . . . well, a little bit . . . opposed to making love with a perfect stranger. Although Derik was far from perfect. "What the hell." She sighed as he bent and nibbled on her throat. "Yes, I am. By the way, I'm on the Pill. And I assume you're disease-free, being a genetically superior irritating being and all."

"The Pill?" He paused in mid-nibble. "Oh. Okay. That's good."

It didn't sound like he thought it was good. In fact, it sounded like he thought it was the opposite of good. "What, you wanted me to get pregnant?" she joked.

"No, no."

Weird. Because he sounded . . . disappointed? Maybe it was a cultural thing. She'd figure it out later.

She slapped a mosquito and kissed him back, delighting in the feel of his hard stomach beneath her fingers, the way his taut muscles rippled under—

"Ouch, damn it!"

"What? What?"

"I'm getting eaten alive, here."

"Yeah, I know," he murmured into her ear. "And if you give me another minute, I'll—"

"I meant by bugs, idiot."

"Oh."

"Where's the Off?"

"Poison in a can? No. No, Sara. Please," he begged as she got up in search of relief. "Don't put that stuff all over you. Please!"

"Derik," she said, exasperated. "I'm going to be one big mosquito bite tomorrow. I'm sorry you don't like the smell, but—"

"Let's go in the truck," he suggested.

She paused and slapped another flying vampire. "Good idea."

In another minute, they were groping and moaning on the front seat.

"Oh, God . . ."

"Um . . ."

"Oh, that's nice . . . here . . . move over here."

"Ah . . . oooh."

"Yeah, like that . . . oh, God."

"Ooooh, baby."

"That's—ow!"

"What?"

"The gearshift is sticking into my neck . . . there. Um. Okay, that's better. Move your hand an inch to the . . . yeah. Oooh."

"Mmm."

"Ow!"

"*What?*"

"Your foot is caught in my shirt."

"Sorry . . ."

"That's better . . . yeah . . . um . . . here, raise up . . . a little more."

"Oh, Christ."

"Yeah."

"Do not stop."

"Well, I don't—ow!"

He sighed. "What?"

"*What*, what? My head is on the floor mat, and you're confused?" She puffed hair out of her eyes, but due to her upside-down position, it just flopped back. "It's a mystery why I'm protesting?"

"Sorry. How's that?"

"Derik, this isn't working."

"What are you talking about?" He was panting, disheveled, bottomless. She would have laughed if she hadn't been so uncomfortable. "It's fine."

"What are you, high? You are, aren't you? And you aren't even sharing the good drugs."

"You're the one with a prescription pad. Besides, you're just not giving it a chance."

"Your *foot* was in my *shirt*. And now I have Raisinettes in my hair."

He burst out laughing. "Okay, okay. You win. Go put the fucking poison on."

"Forget it. Let's just bag it for tonight."

"Aw, man . . ." He indicated his dick, which was happy to see her. "I'm kind of in an awkward situation, here."

"So? Your erection will go away." She grinned. "You know, eventually."

"Aw, Sara . . . you're killing me. I mean, sincerely killing me. I think your luck is going to make my balls blow up."

"Yeah, yeah, cry me a river." She paused. He really did look pathetic. "Maybe I could help you out."

"Please?" he begged.

She wriggled and squirmed around and finally found herself in a position that didn't make her want to scream with pain. She gripped him by the root, pumped up and down, then bent and licked the pearly drop off his tip.

"Oh my God," Derik gasped, his hips thrusting toward her. "Oh, Christ, do *not* stop."

She licked and pumped and licked some more, and then his hand was on the back of her neck and she had a sense of his crushing power, power held in fierce check, heard him moan, "Don't stop . . . don't . . . don't . . ." Then he was pulsing into her mouth.

"Yech!" she said a minute later, while he lay gasping and limp as a noodle—all over. "What have you been eating?"

He rolled his eyes until he was looking at her. "Can't you just let me bask in the moment, here?" he sighed.

"Go jump in the lake," she replied. "Literally."

25

SARA KEPT LOOKING AT HIM OUT OF THE CORNER of her eye, but she did it once too often, because finally Derik said, exasperated, "What?"

"Sorry."

"I can tell you that when I Change, you'll definitely notice. How 'bout that? So stop sneaking looks at me; it's creeping me right the hell out."

"Give me a break," she said, slightly defensively. "It's been a weird week. I can't help being a little nervous."

"Well, don't be. I'd never hurt you."

"No, just kill me."

"Yeah, but it wouldn't have hurt," he said easily.

She could actually feel her eyes bulge in her head as her blood pressure zoomed. "Oh my God, you're serious!"

He just looked at her.

"Okay, well, you can go run off in the woods now," she said. "I'm pissed again."

"In a few minutes." The sky was a gorgeous blaze of pinks and reds—a truly staggering sunset. And she was too annoyed and freaked out to appreciate it. "You okay?"

"Sure. Sure I am." She sneaked a glance at her wristwatch. It had been a long day—she'd spent it staring out the window, at the moon. Last night—heck, the night at Jon's—seemed a thousand years ago.

"Look, you're all set here, right? Just stay with the truck. I'll probably stick close, anyway. Stop looking at your watch, it's making me nuts."

"Sorry," she said, and like a bad dream, her gaze snuck to her watch again. "So, is it, like, *Farmer's Almanac* sunset that you change? Or actual full dark? Because it's a full moon right now, you know."

"I know," he said, and did his voice sound . . . thick? She snuck another glance at him and noted he was staring dreamily at the sky. "Sunset to sunrise. That's when we run with Her."

"Oookay. I'll be cringing in my sleeping bag if you need me." She started toward the truck, and quick as thought, he had her by the arm, gently restraining her. His nails, she noticed with a detachment that was almost like being drugged, were quite long, and curving under.

Sure, it was like being drugged. She was scared, and her brain was trying to help her deal with that fear by going into analyze overload.

Oh, for God's sake, Sara! This was Derik, and bad first impressions aside, he'd chew off his left hand before hurting her.

That was true, and she felt better, even if the sight of those nails—claws, really—was a bit upsetting. "What? What is it?"

"Stay with the truck," he said again, and it *wasn't* her imagination; he *was* speaking with difficulty.

"Okay," she said. "You told me that already, but okay."

Then he was kissing her, almost devouring her, his tongue was in her mouth, and he'd picked her up off her feet, his arms were tight around her back. And he seemed—bigger? Was that possible? Or maybe he just seemed more there, because he was so close to his change.

His mouth moved to her throat . . . and then he abruptly pulled back.

"Well," she said, almost panted. "That was . . . um, interesting. Could you let go of my arm now?"

He did, and was rapidly shedding his clothes, in fact, the only time she saw him undress quicker was when they were about to have sex that first time. Was it only the day before yesterday?

"Easy," she said as the button fly on his Levis went flying. She could hear something—was he grinding his teeth?

No; he was Changing. If she had blinked she would have missed it. He fell to his hands and knees, and his blonde hair grew out, and his fingernails were digging into the dirt of the campsite, and then an enormous wolf was looking up at her, a wolf with fur the exact color of Derik's hair, a wolf with green eyes like lamps in the dark.

The wolf leaned forward, and she bent to it— to him—and he nuzzled her, a quick snuffly kiss, and then she heard the growl ripping out of him and turned so quickly she nearly lost her balance.

There was a smaller wolf at the edge of their camp, hesitating as if sensing the borders of their territory. This one was coal black, with the yellow-gold eyes of a calico cat. And quite small, really very small; Derik quit growling and loped over, and it was shocking how much bigger he was than the other one.

They sniffed each other, and she noticed Derik was at ease with his enormous size, and was trying to put the other one at ease, too. The other one was almost timid, backing off but not running away.

Then she realized: The other one was female. And they were . . . they were going off together! Without so much as a backward look, that fuzzy slut went and nabbed her would-be assassin/ boyfriend/fake fiancé.

"Well, shit," she said, and kicked one of the truck's tires.

DERIK BOUNDED UP TO THEIR CAMPSITE THE NEXT morning, lured by the smell of frying bacon. He was so relaxed, and in such a good mood, it took him a while to realize something was wrong.

He supposed he should have expected it. She *was* human, even if she was an extraordinary one. And he did turn into a wolf in front of her. That was probably pretty weird for her. He'd thought about going off into the woods a good half hour before the sun set to spare her the admittedly odd sight, and in the end he'd shit-canned the idea. Because this was who he was, and if she didn't like it, tough.

But it was more than that: He wanted her to see. See all of him, and not be afraid.

"What's wrong?" he finally asked, deciding to grab the bull by the horns.

"Nothing."

"Oh. Are you, uh, mad about something?"

"No," she lied.

"Oh." Honest to God, he had no idea what to do now. She was lying, and he knew she was lying, and she probably knew he knew she was lying. So what the fuck? "So, uh, everything go okay last night?"

"Fine."

"That's good." Tell her she was lying? Ignore the fact that she was lying? Tell her but at the same time forgive her for lying? Tell a lie himself?

What? "Are you mad because I didn't bring back a rabbit? I thought about it, but to be honest, skinning and cleaning one would be a pretty messy job, and I didn't think you—"

"I really don't care, Derik."

"Oh."

"So," she grumped, poking the fire.

"So, what?" He stretched, feeling pleasantly pooped. "Is there any bacon left?"

"You know damned well there is," she snapped. "Where's what's-her-fur?"

"Huh?" He sat up, puzzled. She wasn't kidding around. Not at all. She was *pissed*. She smelled exactly like the campfire. "What? Did you wake up with a spider on you? *What is it?*"

"That hair-covered-whore you took off with last night, as if you don't remember. That's *what*."

"Hair-covered . . . oh, you mean Mandy?"

"Mandy," she sneered.

"She's not a hair-covered-whore," he said defensively. "She owns her own accounting firm. And she's not here. She went home."

She shook the spatula at him, and he dodged drops of hot grease. "Look, all I want is the truth. Just tell me the truth, okay? I promise I won't get mad."

"But you're already mad," he said, wondering if he could crawl underneath the fire. The truth was, he was sort of morbidly curious . . . what would her powers do to him if she was just mad, but not defending her life? Maybe just give him dandruff, or a sprained ankle. "Really, really mad."

"Oh, shut up. Did you guys do it out there in the woods?"

"Do—oh. Oh!" He laughed out of relief, then dodged as she jabbed the spatula at him. "Sara, for crying out loud. Mandy's *got* a mate. We just paired up to hunt. Remember: Way more of you guys than us. It's really rare to just run into one of us in the woods. So we teamed up. She was on her own, because it was his turn to stay home with the cubs."

"Hmm." She was staring at him with narrowed eyes, but he could tell she felt better.

"I can't believe this! You've been stewing about this all morning?" He was trying to stop laughing; it wasn't likely to make her less mad.

"The most powerful sorceress in the world is jealous of an accountant?"

"M'not jealous," she muttered. "Just wanted to know, is all."

"Well, now you do. And thanks for the vote of confidence, by the way. Yes, we werewolves are so slutty we do it with anything on four legs."

"I didn't mean it quite like that," she mumbled.

"Yeah, sure you didn't."

"Well, I'm sorry," she grumped.

"Besides, I'd never go off with another female now. I'd—" He'd shut his mouth with a snap.

"You'd what?"

"I'd get some of that bacon, like, pronto. I'm starving!"

"And the Universe," Sara said dryly, "realigns itself."

"Seriously," he said after a long moment. "That was really dumb."

"Oh, shut up," she said, but he knew she wasn't mad anymore. Even if she hadn't smelled like roses again, she fixed a whole 'nother pound of bacon, just for him.

26

THEY WERE IN ST. LOUIS, AND TO TELL THE TRUTH, Sara was getting pretty damned sick of the truck. And sick of sleeping outside. And sick of the smell of campfire, how it clung to her hair and clothes and skin.

And really, really sick of bacon. Derik, it appeared, could eat it with every meal. She could not.

But none of that mattered, none of it was important, because, as sick as she was of the whole thing, she didn't want it to end. She wanted to stay like this with Derik—in this adventure limbo—forever.

Because the world would end, or it wouldn't, and either way Derik would be out of her life.

Unacceptable.

That's nice, she told herself. *Put off saving the world so you can get boned a few more times. Very nice.*

"Over halfway there," Derik said.

"Uh-huh."

Right. Because werewolf lovers come along all the time. Why shouldn't I want to hang on to some happiness?

She coughed. "Listen, is there a plan for when we get there? How do we find these guys, anyway? And then what do we do, once we find them?"

"I figured your luck would help us out with finding them. Shit, you'll probably trip and fall on the leader and accidentally give him a fatal concussion. As for the rest of it . . . I can take care of the rest of it."

"You have no idea what the plan is, do you?"

"Never mind," he said primly, which made her laugh.

"It's okay," she said. "We've got some time to work on it, thank God."

"Mmm. Listen, this Morgan Le Fay business . . . maybe if Arthur's Idiots find out you're a good enough gal, they'll stop trying to kill you. I mean, we've only got Dr. Cummings's word for it that they're the bad guys."

"That and what I saw with my own eyes at the hospital," she pointed out.

"Oh, right. Well, like I said, maybe once they find out you're not bad, they'll forget about the whole thing."

"And maybe," she added brightly, "I'll get caught up on my laundry this week. But probably not."

"Seriously. Morgan's whole deal was that she was wicked, bad, blah-blah, but you're not like that."

"Morgan's whole deal, as you so annoyingly put it, is that Merlin set her up, screwed over her family, *splintered* her family, and then took off after he did all that damage."

"Oh." He paused. "Really?"

"Listen, without his interference, she could have been Arthur's greatest champion. She really could have. But she's been totally screwed over, not just by real life but by history, too. Men write the history books," she added neutrally. "So naturally their take on it was that Morgan was this wicked terrible evil witch who destroyed Arthur because she could. But that's not true at all. She was *set up* to destroy him. And then she did. But if things had been different . . ."

"Oh."

"If she'd had a normal family life . . . a normal upbringing . . . who knows?"

"Huh."

"This is the part where you say, 'I never thought about it like that.'"

"Well, I never did."

"Exactly. Men. I mean, I'm not mad about it or anything, because you can't help thinking with your dicks all the time—"

"As long as you're not mad."

"Stop the truck!" she shouted suddenly, and Derik stood on the brakes. Sara was half-strangled by her seat belt, but finally fought free of it and opened her door. She reached back, grabbed the large duffel bag they were using as a communal suitcase, and said, "Come on."

"Come on, what?"

"Trust me."

She ran toward the . . . Amtrak station, Derik belatedly noticed. He ran after her. "A train?" he called. "You want to take a train? Why didn't you say so when we first started seeing trains?"

"I dunno. I'm sick of that truck," she explained, entering the busy station. "And I'll bet you a million dollars we can find a train that goes to Boston. We can ride instead of driving."

"One of us *has* been riding instead of driving."

"That's because you're a wheel hog. You wouldn't let me drive after that one time."

"You can't drive a stick."

"I can, too!"

"So we were stalling all the time, why again? And what are we doing looking for a train?"

"I don't know," she said, "but I think it's going to be all right."

"When we don't have a ticket? What am I saying. The ticket guy won't notice us, or will pretend like we have tickets, because his wife left him this morning, or Amtrak's entire computer system will crash, and they'll be too distracted to worry about two strangers on a train."

"Exactly."

"So, this is like instinct?"

"Exactly."

He was following her past the ticket windows. "Okay."

She turned to look at him over her shoulder. "Really okay?"

"Sure. I'm a huge believer in instinct. Besides"—he smiled at her—"you haven't steered us wrong yet."

27

"YOU KNOW, I COULD GET USED TO THIS," DERIK said, climbing into the sleeping berth beside Sara, who was propped up on one elbow, looking out the window. "No ticket, no money? No problem!"

"I was wondering if it would work," she said, not looking around. "I'm sick of my power—my whatever-it-is—being passive, you know? I wanted to see if I could make it work."

"And you did."

"I *think* I did . . ."

"And say, hon, can you see anything out there?"

"*I* can't," she said, looking over her shoulder

and smiling at him. It was ridiculous what a gorgeous smile she had. "Come here and narrate."

He curled up behind her and peeked over the top of her head, out the window. "Well . . . that's a farm . . . and that's another farm . . . oh, there's a herd of cows, sound asleep . . . mmm . . . cows . . ."

"Don't start, you just ate."

"What, 'just'? Half an hour ago. Oh, now look here, the land's thinning out, probably because . . . yep, there's a river . . . you can see those lights, right? Probably a town right on the river. Where the hell are we?"

"Somewhere in the Midwest."

"Well," he said, nuzzling the back of her neck, "that narrows it down."

"Off my case, hose head, I'm not a walking atlas. You know, this time tomorrow, we could be getting stomped by Arthur's Chosen."

"What a cheerful thought. Thanks for the subject change."

"It could all be over in just another day or two," she said, sounding weirdly neutral. "Just think."

"Yeah. All done. And either the world ends, or we go back to our lives."

"Yeah," she said.

"Um . . . Sara . . . this is going to sound dumb . . . and slightly retarded . . ."

"Thanks for letting me brace myself."

". . . but I'm actually having a great time with you. I—I sort of don't want it to end."

"You asshole," she said, and he was startled to see she was crying.

"What? Jeez, don't do that. I freak out when you do that. Actually, it's the first time I've seen you do that, and I'm definitely freaking out."

"Shut up," she sobbed. "You talk too much."

"Sara, what's wrong? Besides, um, everything."

"That about sums it up," she said, wiping her eyes. "Everything. I don't want it to end, either. I'd rather stay on this train forever than fight and mess up and maybe die, or maybe the world dies, or maybe you die."

"It'll be all right," he said with a total lack of conviction.

"You're a terrible liar. Really. The worst I've ever seen."

"What can I say, we're not bred for it. Not like you guys. You guys are total experts," he said, trying to cheer her up. "Homo sapiens is the most deceitful, rapacious species the planet has ever—"

"Shut up. And have you—have you thought about—I mean, what if you're wrong?"

He snuggled closer to her in the berth. "I have no fucking idea what you're talking about, darling girl."

"Maybe you should kill me tonight," she said quietly, and he nearly fell off the bunk. "Save the world."

"Bullshit!"

"Don't yell, I'm right here."

"You're not evil, Sara. Not even a little bit evil. So how can you destroy the world?"

"What if it's not a conscious act?"

"What if it is?"

"Quit that," she snapped. "We'll get nowhere like this."

"Exactly. So drop it, all right? I didn't go through all this crap to kill you now. Besides," he pointed out, "I probably couldn't, remember? I mean, really couldn't. In addition to feeling just awful about it and not being able to make myself try again."

"Oh. That's true," she said, cheering up. "Your heart would probably explode if you tried."

"Yeah, so quit crying, okay?"

"Shut the hell up and kiss me. Dumb ass."

He did, and she kissed him back, fiercely, almost desperately, and he smelled her fear and anxiety, and soothed her as best he could with his mouth and hands. And after a while, her anxiety gave way to lust, which kindled his own.

They shed their clothes and slid against each other, whispering, nibbling, teasing, sighing, and toward the end, he closed his eyes and breathed her perfume, and they rocked together as the train rolled through the Midwest.

"IF I TELL YOU SOMETHING," HE SAID JUST AS SHE was drifting off, "you have to promise not to get mad."

"Could you sound more like a big girl? What? What is it?"

"You have to promise not to get mad."

"Whenever somebody says that, it's code for, 'you're gonna get mad as hell, so watch out'."

"Yeah, well, you have to promise you *won't* get mad."

"No."

"*No?*"

"That's right."

"Shit. Sara, I've got to tell you this. I mean, it's been, like, haunting me."

"So tell me."

"But I don't want you to get mad," he whined.

"Tough."

"Cripes." He took a deep breath; the berth was so tiny she could feel his chest heave. "Okay. We didn't have to have sex at Jon's. Or the night before, in the woods."

"We didn't have to what what at where?"

"We didn't have to have sex. He knew you weren't really my fiancée."

"And you kept this little tidbit to yourself, because . . . ?"

"Well, because I wanted to get laid," he said reasonably. Then, "Owww!"

"What? I didn't lay a finger on you."

"Oww, damn it, Sara!"

"You jerk! You creep! You ass! Oh, *fuck*!" When she thought of the way she threw herself at him . . . dropping the robe and pulling the quilt back like a big old slut . . . telling herself they were Doing It for a good cause . . . she was furious with embarrassment.

And what did it say about him, that he just boned her and never told her the truth? Other than the fact that he was a lying, sneaking, opportunistic—

"Owwwwww!"

—bastard.

"What are you whining about?" she snapped. "I haven't even gotten started. You son of a bitch! You piece of shit! You—"

"Ow, my fucking sac!" He was cradling his groin and rocking back and forth, as much as their crowded berth would allow. "Sara, will you stop it?"

"Stop what?"

"Calm down," he begged. "For the sake of our unborn children."

"I told you, I'm not doing anything." But was she? She was certainly angry enough to picture a groin-related disaster. Possibly more than one.

Though his yelps of pain were doing wonders for her temper. "Quit complaining."

"Ow, ugh, ow! Oh, man." He moaned piteously. "I think my testicles just imploded."

"Serves you right," she snapped.

"I'm serious, Sara. This is the worst pain I've ever known."

"Good."

"Look, I'm sorry, okay? Really, really, really, really sorry. I was sorry before you blew up my balls."

"I did *not*—"

"It's just, I couldn't have this hanging over us anymore. Especially not after what you said, about how tomorrow might be the big day, you know?"

"So?" she sulked.

"So, I wanted to tell you."

"So, you did."

"Yeah, but you promised not to get mad."

"I did not."

"Okay, well, you got your revenge, right?" He gingerly felt himself. "Oh, boy. I think I'm out of the Sexual Olympics for a while, Sare-Bear."

"Serves you right," she said again, and flopped

over on her side, as far away from him as she could get, which wasn't very far. "Asshole."

"Aw, c'mon," he coaxed. "I said I was sorry. It's not my fault I wanted to fuck you so bad I was willing to—"

"You're not helping your case," she said grumpily, but when he snuggled contritely behind her, she let him.

28

"AH, BOSTON, THE SWEET SMELL OF—SARA, WHAT the *hell*!"

She had tripped, and he was too close on her heels, and went sprawling down the steps and over her. She hit the platform with a thump that made him wince and bit her tongue, hard.

"Oww!" she cried unnecessarily. "I mit my mongue!"

Derik rolled over, quick as a cat. "You what your what?"

"My mongue! I mit it!" She rolled it out, crossing her eyes in an attempt to look at it. "Ith it mleeding?"

"No," he said, pulling her to her feet and ignoring the curious stares of their fellow passengers.

"You nint even look!"

"Sara, if you were bleeding, I'd know it. Now what's the problem?"

"The *mroblem* ith that I nipped over my own two eet an—ow!"

She'd said "ow" because he had grabbed her by the scruff of the neck and hauled her back up onto the train, brutally shoving passengers out of his way and ducking behind the window.

"What? What's wrong? Is it Arthur's Chosen? They're waiting for us, aren't they?" She clawed frantically in her pocket, came up with a Kleenex, dabbed her tongue, checked for blood, then readdressed the situation at hand. "It's them, isn't it? Funny how imminent death totally took my mind off my sore tongue. Which still hurts like hell, FYI. It's the Chosen, isn't it?"

"Worse," he said grimly, peeking out the window. "It's my Pack leader and his wife."

"Really? More werewolves? Oh, that's so cool. And terrifying. Where?"

"Get *down*, idiot."

"Idiot? How'd you like another broken testicle?"

He was ignoring her, peeking out the window. "They're downwind . . . thank God. But how in the hell did they know we'd be here at this particular train station at this particular . . . Antonia."

"I don't think so," Sara said, looking up at him from the floor. "From what you told me, it sounded like she was keeping your secret."

"How else can you explain it?"

"Well. There's me. I mean, my power."

"Maybe." He peeked out the window again. "Is it possible? Would your luck have brought them here? But how come? If Mike sees you, he'll try to kill you, and Jeannie will back him up. I mean, Mike's a toughie, but Jeannie's *insane*, especially when she's knocked up. So why would your luck put you in that position?"

"Are you actually having a conversation with me?" she asked. "Or thinking out loud?"

"It just doesn't make sense," he continued. "The whole point is that we're trying to avoid my Pack. So what would bring them here now, right before we're about to go after the bad guys? Why are they here?"

"Why don't you ask them?" Sara replied. Then she waved, looking past him. "Hi there."

"Don't kill her!" he screeched before he even turned all the way around.

"It's nice to see you, too, Derik," Michael said, yellow eyes glinting in amusement. And . . . something else. Surprise? No. Shock. They were both shocked, and covering.

"Uh . . ."

"This is the part where he says, 'I can explain'," Sara said helpfully.

"I sure as shit hope so," Jeannie said. She was looking bodaciously gorgeous as usual, with that shoulder-length mess of sun-colored curls, freckled nose, and flinty gaze. Terrifying *and* beautiful, the perfect mate for his alpha. Right now she was nervously chewing on her lower lip. "Start talking, or I start shooting."

Sara was slowly getting to her feet. "Did you guys hear all that? You know, what he was babbling while you were walking up to us? Because I'm kind of curious, too. Not that it's not nice to meet you. Because it is, I'm sure. But what brings you here?"

Jeannie and Michael looked at each other, then looked at Sara. "We had to drop off a friend. She doesn't fly. Then I saw you, so we came over."

"That makes perfect sense," Sara said. Derik was amazed; she wasn't scared at all. Meanwhile, his adrenal gland had dumped what felt like about six gallons of fight-or-flight into his system. "I can't imagine werewolves like to fly. Stuck in an iron tube hurtling through space. I mean, it freaks me out to think of it, and I'm not claustrophobic. I don't think."

"Just . . . everybody stay calm," Derik said.

"We *are* calm," Michael pointed out.

"Everybody relax, and I can explain everything."

"Derik, we're fine," Sara said.

"Just, nobody panic."

"What's the matter with you?" Jeannie asked. "You're all twitchy and sweaty. You're usually much more laid back."

"Well. You're armed, which makes me kind of nervous. And, uh, I didn't—we didn't—expect to see you here. Today, I mean. At the train station."

"We didn't expect to see you, either," Jeannie said. "And with a friend." Blond eyebrows wiggled suggestively.

Michael stepped close and sniffed Sara. "A *good* friend," he said.

"Quit that," Sara said, throwing up an elbow. "It creeps me right the hell out."

Jeannie cleared her throat. "Please note how I restrained myself from smelling your butt."

"For which I will be forever grateful," Sara giggled. "Seriously, cut it out." She shoved Michael back, gently enough. "If you want to know something, just ask me."

"Are you Morgan Le Fay?"

"Well, um, yes."

"But she's not evil," Derik said quickly.

"She doesn't smell evil," Michael agreed. He added, "Evil usually smells a little more clove-like. But what I really want to know—"

"*I* want to know why I haven't gotten a hug," Jeannie said, spreading her arms wide. Relieved, Derik stepped close for the embrace, and then

Jeannie's face shot over to the left and the entire
side of his face was numb.

"Ow!"

"That's for putting my kids and husband in
danger while you concentrated on getting laid,"
she snapped, tapping the butt of her Glock.

"Yeah," Michael said, a familiar look on his
face—amusement and disconcertedness. Jeannie
had, literally, beaten him to the punch. "What
she said."

"Hey, working on saving the world here,
okay?" he snapped back, rubbing his sore cheek.

"That's why I didn't shoot you."

"And what 'kids'? There's just Lara, because
you're, like, five minutes pregnant."

"Seven weeks."

"Congratulations," Sara said. "Don't touch
him again."

Jeannie didn't even glance at her. At least she
had taken her hand off her gun and buttoned her
jacket back up, which was always a good sign.
"But Derik, I swear to God, if you put my family
in jeopardy ever again because you've got a personal agenda . . ."

"Ow!"

"Yeah," Michael added, pointing to Derik's face. "Um, there'll be plenty more where that came from."

"Don't *touch* him *again*."

"Or what, Red?" Jeannie asked, supremely unimpressed.

"Or I'll make you eat that Ann Taylor knock-off."

Jeannie gasped. "It's *not* a knockoff!"

"Regardless. Stop smacking him around. If anybody gets to hit him, I do."

"Knock it off. This doesn't have anything to do with you, Red, so pipe down and shut the hell up."

"How about instead I kick your ass up and down the railroad car?"

"I don't know about you," Michael said to Derik, "but I'm experiencing a fantastic degree of sexual arousal."

"I'm too nervous to get hard," Derik muttered back. "Besides, I had kind of a bad night." Then, louder: "Now, ladies, ladies . . ."

"I mean, talk about nerve," Sara was saying. "Sneaking up on us—"

"We walked up to you at five o'clock in the afternoon in broad daylight—"

"And being all annoying and threatening, and all we're doing is trying to save your ass, and everyone else's ass, and we get attitude for it—"

"He's chasing his dick instead of getting down to business! My kids are supposed to come before his sex life. And—and—"

"You never mind about his sex life."

"I will when it's putting my family in danger."

"Well then," Sara snapped back, "you'd better shoot me."

Jeannie blinked.

Derik said, "Don't shoot her."

"I'm waaaiting," Sara sang, folding her arms across her chest.

"Don't shoot her," Michael ordered.

"Aw, can't I? She's so mouthy, it'd be a pure pleasure."

"Look who's talking," Michael muttered, giving his wife a squeeze.

"It won't work, anyway," Derik said. "Don't you think I tried to ice her? It's sort of all tied up in this mess we're in."

"I'm sure I could pull it off," Jeannie announced.

"Try it, you dyed blond homicidal gun-toting weirdo."

"I do *not* dye my hair!"

"Please stop," Derik begged.

"Stop," Michael said, not begging, and Jeannie and Sara both closed their mouths.

"Thank you," Derik said, relieved.

Michael was frowning. "Derik, you think we're here for a reason? For real? Because we thought we were here dropping a friend off because—because of something else."

"Getting to shoot someone," Jeannie added, "would just be icing on the cake."

Sara crossed her eyes at her and stuck out her tongue. Jeannie started tapping the butt of her gun again.

"Why don't we go get a drink, get off this train?" Derik suggested, jabbing Sara in the ribs at the same moment Michael jabbed Jeannie. "Talk about it?"

"Oh, going off and having a drink is your solution for everything," Jeannie snapped.

"It makes a pleasant change from me killing

you, and my wife shooting your friend," Michael said.

"We could do that later," Sara suggested. "If you get, you know, bored."

Jeannie's forehead smoothed out, and she laughed, taken by surprise. Michael just shook his head, smiling.

29

"SO YOU'VE GOT MONEY..."

"Yeah."

"Okay, and you can take our car, we'll grab a rental for the trip back."

"Thanks."

"All right then. Good luck."

"Mike, what's bugging you? It's not me blowing you off."

"No?"

Derik looked over at Jeannie and Sara, who were standing in the doorway of the restaurant, pretending to be polite to each other. Well, it wasn't surprising. In his experience, strong-willed women usually didn't get along. And hardly anybody got along with Jeannie. It was the alpha thing—somebody needed to be in charge. It made her perfect for the Pack, but low on girlfriends. "No. I guess it's pretty bad. I guess you'd better tell me."

Michael hesitated, then plunged. "We were really shocked to see you. Because Antonia . . . Antonia is very upset."

"Upset like screaming foul names upset? Upset like—"

Mike didn't crack a smile. "She said it was too late. She was lying down all morning and then she came to us and said it was too late. That it couldn't be fixed."

"Oh. Well . . . oh."

"Yeah."

"But . . . oh."

"Yeah. So we were all hanging around the mansion waiting for the world to end—"

"I bet that was fun."

"—and Rosie finally said she couldn't take it anymore, that if the world was going to end, she might as well head home for it, so we ran her up here to the train station. It was actually a relief to have something to do."

Derik didn't know what to say. It couldn't be *over*. They hadn't even tried to get the bad guys yet. How could it be over? But Antonia was never wrong.

And now here was his friend, talking about the end of the world like it was a normal everyday thing.

"So," Michael continued, "I'm glad we didn't spend what might be our last day fighting."

"Me, too."

"Good luck," he added with a total lack of conviction.

"Mike," Derik said, then fell silent for a moment. Then, "It'll be all right."

"Yeah?"

"Yeah."

His friend shrugged. Derik still couldn't get over the weirdness of it all. They should be fighting. That's what an alpha did when a Pack member didn't do what he was told—kicked some ass. They should be fighting, and Jeannie should be doing what she did best, which was overreact when her family was in danger, and there should be a brawl right here on Milk Street.

Hell, when you got right down to it, Derik

should have listened to his leader in the first place.

And he didn't really believe it was done, did he? That it was too late? It couldn't be fixed?

"Look," Mike was saying—uh oh, he'd better start paying attention—"you're doing fine so far with all the, uh, ignoring my orders and hooking up with the most dangerous woman on earth—"

"Thanks."

"—but I've just got one piece of advice for you."

"I'm waiting breathlessly, oh, wonderful Pack leader whose lightest utterance gives my life meaning."

"For Christ's sake," Michael muttered. "How does she put up with you? Anyway. The advice is this: Stay focused."

"Stay focused."

"Yeah."

"Okay."

"I'm serious. Keep your eye on the ball."

"It's good that you used a cliché," Derik replied, "or I might not have understood your meaning."

"Just keep it in mind," his friend said, super-mysteriously, which was annoying, but hey, at least they weren't fighting to the death, so that was all right.

"THEY SEEMED NICE," SARA COMMENTED. "FOR A couple of killer werewolf psychos."

"Hey, hey."

"He *did* sic you on me, Derik."

"Yeah, but he didn't know you then."

"What a relief," she said mockingly. "Now I feel so much better. But at least now we know why they were here."

Derik looked at her, which was unnerving, because his pupils were unusually large; the rings of his irises were just thin hoops of green. In fact, ever since Michael and Jeannie had left, he'd been twitchy as hell. Which was making her twitchy as hell. "I know why they were here," he said. "I didn't know you knew."

"It's obvious. Now we have money, and a car, and you're not worried about the Pack sniffing up our backtrail. We can focus on the matter at hand, right?"

"Right," Derik said. "Focus. That's good advice. Actually, the reason they were here was—oh my God!"

"What?" She jerked back and looked around wildly. "What's wrong? It's the bad guys for real this time, isn't it? Get 'em!"

"It's Rachel Ray! Look!"

Sara looked. They had been walking past the New England Aquarium and Legal Sea Foods, and she saw the cameras, the techs, the vans, the wires, and the lights; all evidence of a television show being taped. And in the distance, just disappearing into Legal's, a perfect brunette bob . . .

"Oh my God!" Derik was rhapsodizing. "I can't believe it! Look! They must be doing a show on Boston, or seafood. Or seafood restaurants in Boston." He gripped her arms and shook her like a maraca. *"Do you realize Rachel Ray is in that building less than a hundred feet away?"*

"This is so completely the opposite of staying focused," she informed him.

Incredibly, he was straightening his hair, which was so short it really never got mussed . . . not even after sex! Which was quite a trick. "Do I look okay?"

"You look very pretty, Mabel."

"God, I wish I had my cookbooks with me! I'd have her sign *Thirty Minute Meals Two*." He looked around wildly, as if expecting the book to pop out of nowhere. "Shit! Oh, wait . . . I know! She can sign my shirt." He tugged his T-shirt out of his jeans and smoothed it.

"If you take off the shirt, she can sign your nipple."

He shot her a withering look. "This is serious business, Sara."

It was getting downright impossible not to burst out laughing. "It is?"

"Look . . ." He was holding her fingers, completely unaware that his grip was crushing. Annoying enhanced werewolf strength . . . arrgghh! "I have to do this. I mean, I *have* to. I've been watching her show ever since she started on the Food Network. Both her shows . . . *Thirty Minute Meals* and *Forty Dollars a Day*. She's just the greatest. And I have to find out. This is my chance!"

Sara was having a little trouble following the conversation, which she didn't beat herself up for, because it was pretty bizarre. "Your chance for what?"

"To find out if she's Pack. I mean, she must be.

No ordinary human could be cute *and* charming *and* a great cook *and* do two shows for one network."

"It's a persuasive argument," she admitted.

"But I don't know for *sure*. If I get close enough to smell her, I'll know."

"How can you not know?"

"What, there's a humongous list of were-wolves, and I memorized it?"

"I guess not," she said. "But doesn't Michael know?"

"He won't tell me. I've been after him for years, trying to figure it out, and he won't tell me! Bastard. How do I look?"

"I already told you."

"Okay, well, I'm gonna go do this now." He took a few deep, steadying breaths. "I have to do this."

"I understand." She gestured toward the bright lights. "Go to her."

"Great!" He bent, kissed her, loped off.

Sara watched him go, beyond amused. He was like a kid with a crush. A big, scary kid. She hoped Rachel would be nice to him.

Minutes later, he returned, looking so disappointed she knew at once he hadn't had a chance to meet his idol. "There were too many people around," he said glumly. "I mean, I could have gotten past them without too much—but I didn't want to scare her or make her think I was a stalker or something."

"Maybe next time. Did you find out if she's a werewolf?"

"No. I could smell a Pack member, but I couldn't get close enough to sort it out from the rest . . . it could be a techie, could be her assistant, could be the guy who owns Legal's, for all I know." His eyes narrowed thoughtfully. "But it's gotta be her. It *must* be her."

"Well, you tried."

"Yeah." He looked at her, a serious look. Uh-oh. "Sara, I just wanted to say I really appreciate your support."

"If by 'support' you mean 'mocking you behind your back', then yes, I am chock-full of support."

"No, really, Sara. And I just wanted to say—I mean, to tell you, that maybe when this is all done, we can, you know, hit the road again, maybe try to run into Rachel again."

What an unbelievably weird idea. "Okay. I

mean, that'd be nice. I'd like to do that." As she said the words out loud, she realized it was true. "When this is all done."

He took her hands again, more gently this time, she was relieved to note. "I'm just saying, there's nobody I'd rather follow the *Thirty Minute Meals* show with than you."

"That's . . . so sweet." She bit her lip so she wouldn't laugh. Then, to her total shock—and his, too, she'd bet—she burst into tears.

"Oh, good," he said, hugging her. "Because this is exactly the reaction I was hoping for."

"I'm sorry," she sobbed. "It's just that I want this to be over—over in a good way—so we can do dumb stuff like stalk Rachel Ray. Together."

"Dumb?" Then, "I love you, Sara."

"I love you, too."

He cradled her in his arms. His big, strong arms. She resisted the urge to melt.

"Oh, Derik. How the hell did we get ourselves into this?"

"Who cares? I love you, and we'll fix it. I loved you," he added nostalgically, "from the moment I tried to kill you."

"It took a little longer for me," she confessed.

30

SARA HAD SUGGESTED, IN A PLOY TO DIVERT THEM
from their mission and cheer Derik up, that they
stop by Wordsworth and pick up a new cookbook. Derik agreed at once.

"Is it totally lame that we're putting off going
to Salem?"

"No."

"Well, good." She paused, then walked into
the bookstore as he held the door for her. "Why
isn't it lame, again?"

"We don't even know where we're supposed
to go once we get to Salem," he pointed out reasonably. "Maybe if we keep hanging out, your

power will kick in, or the bad guys will make a move, or something."

"Uh-huh. Is it just me, or has quite a bit of this world-saving trip entailed waiting around for something to happen?"

"It's just you," he said, and trotted toward the cooking section.

"Like hell," she muttered. She had no desire to add to her cookbook collection, but maybe she could check the New Fiction section and see if Feehan had a . . .

Oh. Oh!

After a couple of minutes, she was sitting on the floor in the History section, looking up King Arthur. Which was really kind of silly, after all, she had done lots of papers in school on King Arthur and Morgan Le Fay, so it was unlikely there would be a book here with information she didn't have on—

Arthur's Chosen. Also referred to as Arthur's Sect, Arthur's Guild, and Morgan's Bane. A mysterious sect founded in the year of King Arthur's death, Arthur's Chosen believes Arthur will return one day, but only with the help of his half sister, Morgan Le Fay . . .

Well. That was lucky. She'd just sit here and find out all about the bad guys, thank you very much.

Sara became absorbed.

ONE HOUR LATER...

IDIOT. FUCKING IDIOT!

"You know better," he said out loud, startling the clerk standing a few feet away. He shot her an apologetic grin and followed Sara's scent out the door.

Well, isn't this what you were waiting for? Something to happen?

"Shut up," he said—damn it, he was talking out loud again!

Bad move, bad guys. He could find Sara's backtrail in a snowstorm; he could certainly track her to Salem. And if they harmed *one* hair . . . one *half* of one hair . . . if they touched her . . . *breathed* on her . . . *thought* about her . . .

He noticed people jumping out of his way and supposed he should calm down—he was scaring perfect strangers and really shouldn't growl in public—but he was too fucking annoyed.

THEY WEREN'T IN SALEM. THEY HADN'T EVEN LEFT town. Tracking them—Sara—down had been totally super easy. He supposed he should have been suspicious, but he was too relieved.

He stomped over to the building—an abandoned warehouse near Logan Airport, of course, naturally, it was the sort of thing that all bad guys hung out in, and clearly these bad guys had been watching all the right movies—and was just about to rip the door off its hinges when his cell phone rang.

This was startling, as it hadn't rung since he left the Cape. In fact, most of the time he'd forgotten it was on his hip. He let it charge overnight and clipped it to his belt in the morning and never gave it a thought, just like he never gave pulling on Jockeys a thought. Everybody knew what he was supposedly working on, and no one wanted to bother him. Not to mention, werewolves weren't big on calling each other up and asking about the weather.

So who was calling him? And why now, when he was about to go all Search and Rescue?

He sneezed—the stench of hydrocarbons in the area was really vomit-inducing—and flipped the phone open. Before he could even say hello, Antonia was screeching in his ear.

"Don't do it! Derik, don't go in that building!"

"When this is over," he told her, more than a little rattled, "we have to sit down and talk about how scary you are. You and Sara would get along great, by the way."

"Turn around. Walk away. Leave now. Now!"

"I can't. Sara's in there. I have to go—"

"Shut the fuck up! Derik, if you go in that building, you'll die. I saw it. You'll—" Antonia's voice broke, and he nearly dropped the phone. Antonia? Worked up into tears over *his* ugly ass? "You'll die. Don't go in, Derik. Don't."

"I appreciate the warning," he said. "But I have to. If I don't see you again—"

"Don't!"

"—thanks for all your help."

"You numb fuck! Men! I told Michael it couldn't be taken back, and what does *he* do?

Goes to Boston for a day trip! You guys would think I was, like, wrong occasionally."

"We know you're not wrong," he explained. "But that doesn't mean we're going to lie down and wait for the world to end."

An inarticulate screech was her only answer.

"And thanks for trying to save me. I don't suppose you saw what'll happen to Sara?"

"Ape! Chimp! Gorilla!"

"Now you're just being mean," he said, and closed the phone.

Nuts, he thought. *I forgot to ask her how I die. Well, I suppose I'll find out in a few minutes.*

He was weirdly sanguine about it, and after a moment's thought he knew why. He could face dying, if Sara was all right. He could even face the end of the world, if Sara was all right. But he couldn't stay out in this smelly parking lot and play it safe while the redhead was in trouble.

So, he would go in. And die, because Antonia was never wrong. But maybe Sara would come out of it okay. And maybe not.

It was worth trying, anyway.

He kicked the door off its hinges, belatedly realizing it hadn't been locked. "D'oh!" he said, then picked the door up and sheepishly set it against the wall. "Hello-o?" he called. "You guys better come get me! Quit whatever you're doing to what's-her-name and come on over here. Let's dance."

"Let's dance?" a thrillingly familiar voice said. "That's really bad, Derik."

"Sara!" He avoided three of Arthur's Losers—the cranberry-colored robes were a dead give-away, *why* did they do that?—and ran to her. "Oh, man, thank God you're all right!" He hugged her, lifting her off her feet. Then he shook her. "And what the hell did you think you were doing, going off with the bad guys?" Then he hugged her again. "I don't know what I would have done if something had happened to you, oh, baby, baby." Then he shook her. "Kicked some ass, that's what I would have done! And what is your *problem*? I tell you to stay put, and you leave? Have you never watched a horror movie in your life?" Then he hugged her again. "Oh, Sara, Sara . . . you sweet, sweet dumb ass."

"Will you stop?" She extricated herself with difficulty and puffed a curl out of her face. "I'm gonna throw up if you don't quit that. And I had to go with them."

"What, had to?"

"They said—they said they had snipers. Trained on your head. And I didn't know if it was the truth or a lie. It seemed a little far-fetched. But I know they use guns, because of that time in the hospital—God, was it only earlier this week? I wonder if my car's fixed yet."

"Could you stay focused, please?"

"I *am*. Anyway, I couldn't take a chance. I didn't think you—even you—could survive a head shot. They said if I went with them they wouldn't kill you. So, I went."

"Dumb ass."

"In retrospect, yeah." She lowered her voice, which was stupid, because the Chosen were right there, hearing every word. "They needed my blood." She showed him the inside of her elbow, which had a drop of dried blood on it. "And they didn't even disinfect the needle site. Bastards."

"Your blood? They needed your blood?" That didn't sound good. That didn't sound remotely good. "Like, for to do magic? Like a spell?"

"I've missed their last few meetings," Sara said

dryly, "so I don't know exactly what they need it for."

He put his arm around her, protectively, then turned and glared at the Robed Weirdos. "What's up, fellas? What'd you need her blood for?"

The shortest Arthur's Chosen blinked. "Who are you?"

Derik was almost crushed. These guys clearly had access to powerful magicks, at least one of them could see the future, and they had *no* fucking idea who he was! How totally embarrassing.

"I'm this one's mate, so there," he snapped, squeezing so protectively that Sara yelped. "Oh. Sorry, babe."

"Mate, huh?" Sara muttered back. "Aw. I didn't know you cared."

Weirdly, the robed fellas were bowing. He could smell quite a few more and looked up . . . there were at least a dozen on the catwalk, and even more in the back where he couldn't see. They were *all* bowing.

"Why are you doing that?" Sara asked, and he was so puffed up with pride—she didn't sound afraid at all, though he knew perfectly well she was—that he almost squeezed her again. "I don't think you should do that. Do you think they should do that, Derik?"

"Definitely not."

"You are our sworn enemy," they all said in unison. Then the one who had spoken first added, "But you are also the daughter of a king, and the sister of a king."

"Um . . . I'm the daughter of an ad exec, and the sister of nobody," Sara said. "But, thanks anyway."

"In *this* incarnation," one robed fella said.

"And I'm not going to destroy the world," she added, "and you can't make me!"

"Darned right you're not," another of the Chosen said. "Why do you think *we're* here?"

"To, um, kill me?"

"To try," Derik added silkily, in his turn.

"We knew you were coming. Did you think we weren't ready? We've had years to arm ourselves with formidable magicks."

"Whoa, whoa." Sara made the time-out sign with her hands. "The only reason I'm here is because your Chosen Ones showed up at my hospital! My mentor told me all about you and sent us to Massachusetts. If you hadn't tried to kill me, I'd still be in California."

"I'm such a loser," Derik muttered in her ear. "Because that actually depressed the shit out of me. We'd never have met!"

"Stop thinking with your dick," she hissed back.

"Your mentor is a traitor to our cause and will be killed on sight . . . as soon as we attend to this other business."

Sara gaped. "Dr. Cummings was one of you?"

"Used to be one of us. Then we discovered he was a foul traitor."

"He was only using us to get information for one of his doctorates," another one explained. "He didn't care about our cause."

"Yeah, that sounds about right," Sara agreed. "He's really aggravating that way."

"Nice of him to warn us, though," Derik said.

"Extremely nice." Then Sara added, "Besides, I can't do magic. I don't know any spells, or anything. I'm a nurse, for God's sake!"

"Then, as a nurse," one of them said from the catwalk, "you know that sometimes it's necessary to hurt a patient to heal another one."

"Uh . . . we're talking theoretically here, right?"

"Your blood will bring back His Majesty, King Arthur. Without your interference, *woman*"—he spat that word out like someone else would have said "child molester"—"he will be the greatest of all of us. He will raise Britain to heights only dreamed of. He will . . . *not! Be! Dead!*"

"Oh, boy," Derik muttered. "Someone forgot their meds today."

"Probably more than one day," Sara said. Then, louder: "You mean you're not going to make me destroy the world? You're going to use my blood to—I dunno—clone or resurrect a new Arthur?"

"Well, sure," another robed one said, one not quite so frothy at the mouth. "What'd you think we were going to do?"

"But Sara doesn't do magic," Derik said. "In case you guys weren't listening the first time."

"That's a relief," the mellower one said. "It makes this all so much easier."

A few of the robed fellows in the corner, who had been bustling busily about during their conversation, now revealed the small lab table where they'd been working. Evil-smelling smoke was pouring from various beakers. It's color exactly matched the cranberry of their robes!

"They don't know about your luck," Derik whispered. "How can they not know?"

"Shit, Derik, *I* didn't know until a few days ago. But how are they going to make Arthur just appear? Even if they cloned him, somehow, he'd have to grow. He wouldn't just appear—"

"We can hear you, you know," one of them said. "I mean, you're only standing ten feet away."

"Aw, shut up," Derik said.

"Arthur—the dead king Arthur—can't just appear," Sara was reasoning out loud. "It doesn't make sense. Unless—"

"Doseda nosefta kerienba!"

"—unless they know some sort of magic spell," she finished, and sighed. "Magic. Cripes! I'm from California, and I still don't believe it. Oh, yuck! Look. They're splashing my blood all over the table. Gross! And I don't see a single biohazard sign, thank you very much."

"Uh, if you don't need any more of her blood—"

"Yes, yes, you're free to go," one of them said, without looking up.

Derik and Sara looked at each other.

"Seriously?" Sara finally asked.

"Yes, yes. Go."

"Go as in *leave?* Or go as in wait quietly in the corner for you to come over and kill us with an axe?"

"This makes *no* sense," Derik said. "You tried to blow her brains out at the hospital, but now she can leave?"

"We just needed some blood to complete the spell," Surprisingly Reasonable Robed Guy explained. "It was the last thing. We've spent years collecting the other ingredients. And she *is* a foul sorceress. We didn't want to take any chances."

"Which, since she accidentally killed all the bad guys, wasn't the worst plan, I suppose," Derik said grudgingly.

Surprisingly Reasonable Robed Guy shrugged. "That was mostly Bob's plan."

"So we're *leaving?*" Sara blurted. "We can just go?"

No answer. The robed ones all took turns muttering chants and moving things around on the lab table. Sara pointed to the pentagram outlined in what looked like green chalk, which she had just noticed.

"I have to admit," Derik admitted, "I didn't really see this coming."

"What do we do?" Sara asked, gripping his hand. "Do we leave? We can't just leave. Can we?"

"I . . . guess not."

"We didn't travel all the way across the country so they could snatch a few cc's of my blood and then kick us out. *We're* the good guys. *We're* supposed to save the world from *them*!"

"Hey, Sara, I'm with you, okay? What do you suggest?"

"We stop them from the spell they're working on!"

"I don't know if messing with them when they're in the middle of performing black magic is the best idea . . ."

"True, but I don't think anything good can come from trying to raise the dead. It's, like, a philosophy of mine."

"Even if it is King Arthur who, you gotta admit, would be kind of cool to talk to. Okay.

You stay here. On second thought, you come with me. Maybe if they try to stab me, you can give them a brain-bleed or something." He gripped her hand, then loosened his grip when she yelped again, and started forward. "Hey! You guys! In the robes! Stop what you're doing!"

31

"MODESA NOEKA BIRIENZA DOSEDA NOSEFTA KE-
rienba modesa noeka—"

"That's totally the opposite of stop what you're doing," Derik said, and Sara almost laughed. What a day. What a week! Nothing was turning out the way she had expected. Was that a good thing, or a bad thing?

A bubble, poison green and clear as glass, rose from the table, enveloping the chanters as it grew. With every spoken word, it got bigger. There was no pain when it enveloped her and Derik, and no smell. Suddenly, the world was green, and the bubble was still growing.

Derik rushed forward, tossing robed fellows

like red checker pieces, and as she hurried to help him, the lab table fell over. The screams of the Chosen Ones almost drowned out the glass breaking.

The world was still clear green—it was like being trapped inside a mucous bubble—but now an ominous humming had started. Sara clapped her hands over her ears—the sound was so low it made her teeth hurt—but the sound went on, and she realized it was going on inside her head.

"We did not finish! We did not finish!"

"Let me guess," she said, taking her hands down—what was the point? "That's bad."

"The moGhurn! The moGhurn!"

Derik was standing, brushing glass and blood off his T-shirt. "What the hell is a moGhurn? And where are all of you guys going?"

There was something in the bubble with them. It was so sudden . . . one minute there was breaking glass and pandemonium and yelling, and the next she felt so heavy she had trouble breathing. The air had gotten heavier, or—it sounded dumb, but—her spirit had gotten heavier. Something had appeared, had been conjured up out of blood and despair and desperate hope, something the sect was trying to run from, but they were all trapped in the green bubble together.

The moGhurn looked like a devil crossed with an elm tree. It had a face, of sorts, and eyes and arms, and was terrible, all terrible—she could think of nothing good to describe it. It swept up members of the sect in its—arms?—branches?—and dashed them to the ground, or pulled their limbs off like her mother used to pull the leg off a chicken, and for a funny thing, it made much the same sound, the sound of gristle tearing and parting from meat, and then she bent, and stared at the green floor, and worked hard on not throwing up.

In the panic she had been separated from Derik, but now the dead gaze of the moGhurn fell on her, and it moved toward her with the rapid, inhuman speed of a snake. She backed up as far as the bubble would let her and she saw . . .

. . . she saw . . .

She saw the sect killed, all of them, heaps of robes everywhere. She saw Derik, dead. She saw the moGhurn reach for her, and then the bubble burst in a feat of amazing and unlikely luck—and the moGhurn, delighted to be free, forgot about her and moved out into the world.

The moGhurn killed everyone in the Boston area, from the oldest man in the Chelsea nursing home, to the infant girl who was born forty minutes ago. This took the demon about two and a half hours. In a day, it had finished with Massachusetts; in a week, the Eastern seaboard. The more it destroyed, the stronger it grew—no magical green bubble to keep it in check any longer—and in a month, North America was gone.

Except for her. Lucky, lucky Sara, spared by the moGhurn, who was distracted at exactly the right moment.

And in another thirty days, she was alone. She was alone in the world. She had not meant to, but everyone was dead all the same, and the moGhurn was still hungry . . . this time, Morgan Le Fay had triumphed, and her reward was a dead world.

Sara blinked, and the bubble was back. There were still bad guys running around in robes—though quite a few of them were dead. Derik was punching the bubble, trying to get out. Everything was green.

She groped, saw what she wanted, leaped for it. An empty hypo amid the broken glass and blood. She pressed the plunger, then pulled it back. Right in the heart. Instant embolism. No more luck. MoGhurn stays put. *Good-bye, cruel world. Oh, Derik, and you'll never know how brave I was.*

Do embolisms hurt?

No time like the present to find out. She slammed the needle forward, gritting her teeth, and then—

"Ow!"

Derik's hand, protectively across her chest. Goddamn it! That spooky werewolf speed could be a real pain in the ass sometimes.

"Derik, you idiot!" she shouted. "I have to!"

He jerked the needle out of the back of his hand, then tossed it. "Like hell!" he shouted back. "Bad, bad, bad, *bad* plan. Bad Sara! No suicides today, please. If this fucking weird green circle thing ever breaks, you run like hell, Sara." He kissed her hard, then thrust her back. "Run!"

She wanted to scream after him but didn't have the breath—it had been knocked out of her by what she was seeing. Derik was running right for the moGhurn, knocking Chosen Ones out of the way like bowling pins.

"We're supposed to be scared of a mutated oak tree?" he shouted, then leaped for the demon, who caught him and shook him like a doll.

Shook him like a *doll*?

Her Derik?

Her Derik?

"Get your tree limbs off him!" she roared, stomping toward the demon. "You piece of shit! You overgrown nightmare from a Tim Burton movie! You leafy motherfucker! *Let him go or I will kill you, I swear it, I swear it!*"

She stomped through broken beakers, barely feeling the glass slice through her sneaker, her sock, her foot. "Right now! Not tomorrow now, not an hour from now, *now,* now!"

It towered over her, and Derik was dangling, limp, from its awful grip. She was afraid, but on top of the fear was anger—true, dark anger, that anyone, anything should treat her love like that. The moGhurn tossed Derik aside like an empty milk carton, and she saw red. Literally, saw red. It was reaching for her and she knew she was no match for it, knew it would kill her—*but that was okay because it looked like Derik was dead, too, so who cared?*—and she did the only thing she could as it bent toward her: She kicked it.

It screamed—horrid, awful, terrible noise—and staggered away from her. This was gratifying, if startling. It screamed, and screamed and shook, and knocked over Robed Ones, and ran around like an evil leafy tornado, and fell over, and twitched like it was being chopped down by a chainsaw, and then it shrank down into itself and disappeared.

Then the bubble popped, and she realized her foot hurt like hell, was, in fact, bleeding pretty good.

"Who cares?" she muttered, racing over to Derik, who was lying in the corner all crumpled and banged up. She skidded to her knees beside him, hesitated,

I could . . . I could . . . I could hurt him more by moving him

and then turned him over. He came into her arms with a loose, boneless feel that scared her worse than the tree demon had.

"Derik," she said softly, and cried at his dear,

battered face, the way his head was tipped too far back in her arms—broken neck at the axis for sure, maybe the atlas as well—and the blood, all the blood. His eyes were open, but he wasn't seeing her. She groped for a pulse, found nothing. Nothing. "Oh, Derik, you big dumb ass . . . you weren't supposed to die. Me, okay, and the rest of the world—a faint possibility. But not you. Never you."

He's only clinically dead, you dumb ass! What, you've got no training? Get to work!

But his neck . . . his neck was . . .

Get to work!

Right. She set him down on the cement floor and started a closed chest massage. One and two and three and four. One and two and three and four. *Oh, don't be dead. Don't.* One and two and three and four. *Oh, don't you dare leave me. Don't you dare. Like I could settle for an ordinary guy after this. Don't.* And one and two and three—

"Sara . . ."

"Now I'm alone," she panted. And two and three and four. "Alone with a zillion people in the world, and where the hell am I going to find someone else like you?"

"Sara . . ."

"What?" she wept. She stopped pumping and pulled him back onto her lap. "What, idiot?"

"Where's the bad guy?" The whites of his eyes were blood red, and blood was even leaking from his left eye like dark tears.

"I kicked him and he died," she sobbed.

"Way to make . . . make a guy feel . . . useful," he gasped, and coughed, and now there was more blood, oh, God, like there wasn't enough before.

"Does it hurt?" she cried. Probably not, she realized clinically; shock would keep much of the pain at bay.

"It's pretty fucking excruciating," he admitted.

"It is? Oh my God, Derik, I'm so sorry, let me go pull some robes off these dead idiots, you must be freezing."

"I just want a drink," he groaned. "Possibly ten. Help me up."

She almost burst into fresh tears—he had no idea how badly he was hurt. How he had minutes, at the most, to live. How he had already died, and she'd only brought him back through luck and some brute skill. The damage she could see was bad enough—she couldn't imagine what had happened internally. Crushed liver. Collapsed lungs—it was a wonder he had the breath to talk at all. *Oh, Derik.* "Just—just lie still and the ambulance will come."

"Sara, it stinks in here, I've had a bad day, and I'd really like to get off this disgusting floor," he snapped. "Help me up."

"Just lie still, Derik," she soothed.

He rotated his neck on his shoulders, irritably, like a man trying to work out a kink. She heard the crackling sound of air popping free of bones, and then he coughed again, wiped the blood off his chin with a grimace, and sat up in her arms. His left eye was still bloodshot. The right was entirely clear.

"What a dump," he said in disgust, looking around the chaos of dead bodies, scorched robes, broken glass, upended tables. "What a day! Let's get the hell out of here. Stop it, that tickles."

She was feeling him all over. "Oh my God. Oh my God! So quick, it was so quick!"

"Yeah, well, superior life form, baby. I told

you this already." He rubbed the eye that was still bloody, and when he quit she saw that it was now clear. "Doesn't hurt that the full moon's not that far behind me. And I think you had something to do with it, too."

"Me?" she gasped, feeling him.

"Yeah, I wouldn't be able to heal this fast normally. I think your power—your sorcery—I dunno, wrapped me up in a magical envelope, or whatever."

"Really? Let's consider this caref—"

"Later. Cripes, I'm sore. What a day."

"Shut the hell up." She put her thumbs on his lower lids and pulled them down. The sclera of both eyes were a perfectly healthy pink. "I can't believe it, I can't believe it! It was so fast!"

"Like I said. I think I've got you to thank for that. I mean, I'm a fast healer, but that was extra special. Maybe your power sort of wrapped me up, like a lucky hug. Or something." He grinned. "*I'd* hug you, but first I need a new shirt. And possibly new underpants—that tree demon thingy was scary."

"What about Arthur's Chosen?" she asked, almost whispered. She'd never been in a room full of dead bodies before—not since nursing school.

"What about 'em? They're all dead. *Luckily*, the demon killed them all, and then you fucked him up before he could do anything else."

"You're right," she said after a minute. "I *am* scary."

"Scarier than taxes, babe."

He took her hand and led her from the warehouse she'd honestly thought was to become her tomb.

PART THREE

Mates

PART THREE

32

"I GUESS THE QUESTION, 'WILL THEY BE SURPRISED to see us?' has been answered," Sara commented as they pulled up to Wyndham Manor. A huge banner reading GOOD WORK SAVING THE WORLD was strung across the front entryway.

They got out of the car, just as a dizzying parade of people poured out of the doors of the house—mansion, really. Sara found herself picked up and hugged by Michael and several other ridiculously good-looking men she'd never met before. Jeannie was kissing and hugging Derik, and a petite, stunning blonde was climbing all over him like a monkey, laughing and say-

ing over and over again, "You did it! I can't believe you did it!"

Then intros: Michael and Jeannie (whom she
already knew), and their daughter, Lara, who
had her father's odd yellow brown eyes and her
mother's aggressiveness, and the petite blonde
was Moira, and oh, several others that she lost
track of, but she didn't mind, because even
though they were all strangers, it was exactly like
coming home.

"SO YOU TOLD THEM WE WERE COMING, HUH?"
Derik asked.

Antonia, who was just as ridiculously breath
taking as the rest of them, shrugged. "Don't get
pissy. It's what I do."

"Thanks for all your help," Sara said.

Antonia grunted. Sara had never known that
someone who looked like a swimsuit model
could be so sullen.

"So, what's next for you two?" Jeannie asked,
picking up the pitcher of lemonade, pouring herself a glass, then promptly draining it off. They
were sitting in a gorgeous sunroom, the remains

of a glorious lunch laid out before them. "And why did I do that?" she griped aloud. "Like I don't have to pee often enough. Pregnancy," she finished in a mutter.

"You're glowing," Michael said automatically.

"That's because of all the puking," she retorted.

"So?" Michael prompted. "You guys? What's next?"

"Um . . ." Sara said, because she didn't have a clue.

"Well, we're getting married in a couple of days, and Mike's going to give us an RV for a wedding present, and then we're going to drive around the country looking for Rachel Ray."

"That's the lamest marriage proposal ever," Sara commented, while Antonia actually cracked a smile.

"Yeah, but you're gonna go along with it." When she didn't say anything, he dropped the cocky pose. "Right, Sara? Sara? Right? You're gonna be my mate, right? Sara?"

"Oh, Christ, tell him yes," Antonia said, rolling her great dark eyes. "Before I pick up this fork and jam it into my ear, just so I don't have to listen to any more of that."

"Actually, it's a refreshing change," Michael commented, biting the chicken leg in half and sucking out the marrow in one slurp. Sara managed to conceal her shudder. "Keep him on the hook, Sara."

"Never mind," she told them, and then said to Derik, "It would have been nice to have been asked, jerk. But it sounds like a fine plan."

"Congratulations," Antonia said, bored. Then she leaned forward and speared Derik with her gaze. "And before I forget, numb nuts, who told you to go to her house and kill her?"

"Huh? I mean, you did."

"No, I told you to *take care of her*. As in, look out for her, so she could destroy the moGhurn when it manifested."

"*What*? Wait just a goddamned minute! You *never* told me to look out for her. You told me—"

"Well, I knew you wouldn't be able to ice her, but I wanted you to stay close anyway," Antonia explained. "The world was saved because you were fated to love her, not because you were fated to kill her. Not to mention, you were fated to die . . . but not for too long. Dumb ass."

"Now *wait one minute*." Derik was as furious as Sara had ever seen him. She clutched at his sleeve, trying to get him to sit down, but he towered over Antonia and ignored Sara's tugging. "You sent me there to—"

"Take care of her—do I have to get out the hand puppets? Look, Derik, I couldn't tell you the whole thing. We probably wouldn't be sitting here right now if you'd known what I'd known. Not that you could ever be bright enough to know what I know—"

"God*damn* it, Antonia!"

"Oh, take a chill pill. Everything that happened this week, you guys had to do. It *all* led to the big showdown. High noon in Boston, so to speak."

"I still don't get it," Sara confessed. "The bad guys—Arthur's Chosen—made the demon-thingy on purpose? No?"

"No, it was an accident. You screwed up the spell. They were trying to bring Arthur back, remember? With your blood. But the spell screwed up—which anybody who watches *Charmed* will tell you—and then they were in over their heads. I mean, that's the trouble with screwing around with black magic. You make one slip, and suddenly there's a world-devouring demon in your warehouse."

"Which Sara got rid of," Derik said, calming down. "You guys shoulda seen it."

Sara laughed, which calmed Derik down even further. "I was so scared, I didn't know what to do. I think I kicked it—the whole thing's kind of a blur. I guess my blood did away with it? Because my blood conjured it up?"

"Do I look like I'm wearing a pointy Merlin hat?" Derik griped. "Track down your mentor, Dr. Cummings. Ask him. He can probably explain the whole thing."

"And this whole 'everything is for a reason' bushwah . . . you mean my car conking out was part of the big plan, too?"

"The universe is a mysterious place," Antonia said, popping the last cherry tomato into her mouth.

Derik sat down. "Fucking miracle it all turned out all right," he muttered. *"Miracle."*

"Oh," Sara said, leaning forward and kissing him on the cheek. "My specialty."

"At least the alpha thing is taken care of," Moira said. "Thank God."

"What alpha thing?" Sara asked.

"It doesn't matter now," Derik said, visibly uncomfortable.

"What?" Michael said. "It's fine, Derik. Shit, I'm not one to argue fate." He glanced fondly at his wife. "Not anymore."

"What are you guys talking about?" Sara asked.

"Derik's an alpha, too, which usually means trouble for us," Moira explained, "because our Pack already has an alpha."

"I don't suppose he can, like, try to win the next alpha election, or whatever . . ."

"It doesn't exactly work like that," Antonia said dryly.

"But part of the problem of *being* alpha is the overwhelming urge to *prove* it . . . men," Moira added, shaking her head.

Sara decided she would like the tiny blonde, if the woman wasn't so damned cute. Thank God she was married!

"Anyway, not only does Derik not have to prove anything," Moira went on, "he's aligned himself with a mate who is quite possibly the most powerful being on the planet."

"Oh, now, well," Sara said self-deprecatingly.

"Know anybody else who can get rid of a demon by kicking it?" Antonia asked rudely.

"Kicking it," Jeannie said, shaking her head. Then, "Excuse me. I gotta pee."

"Anyway," Moira continued, frowning at Antonia, who sneered back, "it sounds like you guys aren't even going to be around that much. So the problem has, essentially, been solved. Both internally—feeling alpha and feeling the need to prove it—and externally, because you'll be traveling."

"Oh," Sara said. It all sounded like a lot of werewolf bullshit to her. She'd have Derik go over it with her later. Probably. "Well, that's good."

"Real good," Michael said, "because I would have broken out all his teeth, and then I really would have gone to work on him. And I would have hated to do that."

"Dude, what have you been sniffing? You

were so *toast* if I decided to bring the smack-down. I would have spanked you!"

"And then I would have snapped your spine."

"You're high! You are on *serious* uppers, dude! You gotta know I would have totally . . ."

"God, I'm bored," Antonia mumbled. "At least when we thought the world was gonna end, it was interesting around here."

"Maybe you can go off an have an adventure of your own," Sara suggested.

"Yeah, yeah . . ."

"So," Sara said to Jeannie, who had just re-turned and was working on her third glass of lemonade, "how are you feeling?"

"Oh, fine. I haven't started craving raw meat yet—thank heavens."

"Are you thinking about names?"

Jeannie set down her glass and shook her blonde hair out of her face. "Well, you know, Sara," she said seriously, "we really haven't been lately. Because of—because we weren't sure what was going to happen."

"Oh. Sure, I get it."

"But I guess now we have to get back to it.

And I think, just for the record, that Sara is a lovely name."

"Oh, vomit," Antonia said, which was just as well, because Sara was too choked up to say anything.

EPILOGUE

"HI, AND WELCOME TO 'FORTY DOLLARS A DAY.' I'M
Rachel Ray, and I'm here today at the annual San
Antonio rattlesnake festival with Derik Gardner,
who has taken first prize with his *wonderful* dish,
Rattlesnake *en croûte*. I know, I know, it sounds
kind of yerrrgggh, but you *gotta* try it. Derik has
come out of *nowhere* and unseated last year's
champion with his awesome dish. Derik, congratulations!"

"Thanks, Rachel."

"Your dish is *delicious*. I mean, yum! Who
would have thought something made out of
snake could look so delicious? I mean, look at
that, so crispy and golden and just . . . gorgeous!
And it's very tender. It really doesn't taste like

chicken at all. So, Derik, do you catch the rattle-snakes yourself?"

"Yes, I do, Rachel."

"That's *amazing* . . . do you use a net, or a trap?"

"Something like that, Rachel."

"And this is your wife? Sara?"

"Yeah, hi."

"Do you help Derik catch the rattlesnakes?"

"God, no. The whole thing just creeps me out. I stay in the RV, while he does that."

"Well, it looks like you get to partake in the fruits of his labor, then . . ."

"Yes, lucky me."

". . . and is it true you two travel around the country going to cooking shows and the like?"

"Yes, that's true, Rachel."

"Well, that's certainly working out well for you so far, at least from where I'm standing."

"Thank you, Rachel."

"You're right about that one, Rachel."

"Oh, whoa now! I guess you would call that the newlywed effect . . . and congratulations, by the way."

"Thanks, Rachel."

"Yeah," Derik said, beaming. "Thanks."

Continue reading for a special preview of
MaryJanice Davidson's next novel

Undead and Unappreciated

Look for the hardcover coming soon
from Berkley Sensation!

"OKAY, GUYS, LET'S SET UP HERE...CHARLEY, YOU okay here? You got light?"

Her cameraman looked up. "It's shitty out here. Should be better inside."

"We won't film out here ... So, you're sure this is okay?"

The representative, who was smooth and sweatless, like an egg, clasped his hands together and nodded slowly. Even his suit seemed to be free of threads or seams. "People need to see that it's not a bunch of chain-smoking losers who are afraid to go outside. There's doctors. There's lawyers. There's"— he stared at her with pale blue eyes—"anchorwomen."

"Right, right. And we'll put all that across." She turned away from the AA rep, muttering under her breath. "Fuckin' slow news days . . . okay! Let's get in there, Chuckles."

Charley knew his stuff. With the new equipment, setup was not only a breeze, it was relatively quick and quiet. Interestingly, none of the room's inhabitants looked at them directly. There was a lot of coffee drinking and low chatting, a lot of nibbling on cheese and crackers, a lot of quiet milling and sideways glances. They looked, the newswoman thought to herself, exactly like the man said. Respectable, settled. Sober. She was amazed they'd agreed to the cameras. Wasn't the second *A* supposed to be for *Anonymous*?

"Okay, everyone," the rep said, standing in the front of the room. "Let's get settled and get started. You all remember Channel 9 is here tonight, to help raise awareness . . . someone watching tonight might see we're not all villains in trench coats and maybe will come down."

"I left my trench coat in my other pants," someone called in a low voice, and the room rustled with restrained laughter.

"Anyway, I'll start, and then we've got a new person here tonight . . ."

Someone the reporter couldn't see protested in a

low voice, and was ignored—or wasn't heard—by the rep. "I'm James," he said, "and I've been sober for six years, eight months, and nine days."

There was a pause as he stepped down, then a rustle, a muffled "Oof! Stupid steps" and then a young woman in her mid-twenties was standing behind the small podium. She squinted out at the audience for a moment, as if the fluorescent lighting hurt her eyes, and then said in a completely mesmerizing voice, "Well, hi. I'm Betsy. I haven't had a drink in three days and four hours."

"Get on her!" the reporter hissed.

"I'm tight," Charley replied, dazzled.

The woman was tall—her head was just below the No Smoking On These Premises sign—which put her at about six feet. She was dressed in a cherry red suit, with the kind of suit jacket that buttoned up to her chin and needed no under blouse. The richly colored clothing superbly set off the delicate paleness of her skin and made her green eyes seem huge and dark, like leaves in the middle of the forest. Her hair was golden blond, shoulder length, and wavy, with red and gold highlights that framed her face. Her cheekbones were sharp planes in an interesting, even arresting face.

Her teeth were very white and flashed while she spoke.

"Okay, um, like I said, I'm Betsy. And I thought I'd come here . . . I mean, I saw on the Web that . . . Anyway, I thought maybe you guys would have some tricks or something I could use to stop drinking."

Dead silence. The reporter noticed the audience was as rapt as Charley was. What presence! What clothes! What . . . were those Bruno Maglis? The reporter edged closer. They were! What did this woman do for a living? She herself had paid almost three hundred bucks for the pair in her closet.

"It's just . . . always there. I wake up, and it's all I think about. I go to bed, I'm still thinking about it."

Everyone was nodding. Even Charley was nodding, making the camera wobble.

"It just . . . takes over. Totally takes over your life. You start to plan events around how you can drink. Like, if I have breakfast *here* with my friend, I can hit an alley afterward *there*, while she's going uptown. Or, if I blow another friend off for supper, I can reschedule on *him* and get my fix instead."

Everyone was nodding harder. A few of the men

appeared to have tears in their eyes! Charley, thankfully, had stopped nodding, but was getting in on the woman as tightly as he could.

"Get the suit in the shot," the reporter whispered.

"I'm not used to this," the woman continued. "I mean, I'm used to wanting things, but not like *this*. I mean, gross."

A ripple of laughter.

"I've tried to stop, but I just made myself sick. And I've talked to some of my friends about it, but they think I should just suck it up. Ha ha. And my new friends don't see that as a problem at all." More nods all around. "So here I am. Nobody special. Just someone with a problem. A *big* problem. And . . . I thought maybe coming here and talking about it would help. That's all." Silence, so she added, "That's really all."

Spontaneous, almost savage, applause. The reporter had Charley pan back, getting the crowd's reaction. She wasn't sure the rep would let all their faces be shown on the ten o'clock news, but she wanted the film in the can, just in case.

She wanted Charley to get the woman walking to

the back of the room, but when he panned back, she was gone.

The reporter and her cameraman looked for the gorgeous stranger for ten minutes, with zero luck.

Gone.

Shit.